In remembrance
Of
Debbie Blankenship

Cougar Woman
(Unabridged Edition)

Cougar Woman

(Unabridged Edition)

JANE E. HARTMAN

FOREWORD BY JOSEPH EARL RAEL

AQUARIAN SYSTEMS INCORPORATED
PUBLISHERS
PLACITAS, NEW MEXICO

Published by: **Aquarian Systems Incorporated, Publishers**
PO Box 575
Placitas, NM 87043

Front cover original art by Dee Lambert
Edited by Ellen Kleiner
Book design by Richard Harris
Cover design by Janice St. Marie

An abridged edition of this book was published in 1983 by Sunstone Press in Santa Fe, New Mexico.

Printed in the United States of America

Publisher's Cataloging-in-Publication Data

Hartman, Jane E.
    Cougar Woman / Jane E. Hartman. — Unabridged ed.
    p. cm.
    ISBN O-9618045-1-3

    1. Crow Indians—Fiction. 2. Historical fiction. I. Title.

PS3558.A7124C68 1997   813'.54
                                          QBI96-40306

10 9 8 7 6 5 4 3 2 1

To Jean, Ann, and Helen
for soul support, encouragement,
and gifted editorial help

Contents

Foreword

Cougar Woman does not see power outside of her but lives it. She learns to ride the top currents of the ocean of action and learns that thought and executing it go together.

On her path she meets the totality of her being in people like Bold Eagle, Tall Bull, and Dreaming Boy, and in all the things that she feels, thinks, and does.

Dr. Jane E. Hartman brings together a group of meaningful Native American practices which creatively reveal the gift of womanhood—that Wisdom and Intelligence when empowered do lead to knowledge of truth. That lifestyle, in order to be a successful one, must assimilate the laws of abundance, of selection, of preservation, and of active contribution.

Yes, it is true, *Cougar Woman* is the manifestation of Divine Law and what our roles in it can be.

Joseph Earl Rael, MA
Beautiful Painted Arrow
Picuris Pueblo and Southern Ute Indian
Originator of Peace Chambers throughout the world

Preface

To bring *COUGAR WOMAN* to life in its unabridged form took some soul-searching. In the end I agreed to it for several reasons. First, because the need for strong heroines in literature is at least as pressing now as it was in 1983, when the condensed version of this book came to print. Second, because the lives of Native American women remain too often uncelebrated. And third, because the condensation of the original manuscript excluded events essential to the integrity of the story.

The missing pieces have been reintegrated—and fortunately so, for they may help address the rapidly expanding interest in Native American life we have witnessed in recent years. People of all ages and ethnic backgrounds are now studying, if not emulating, traditional Indian lifestyles and values. Native peoples, we are learning, did not attempt to destroy or master nature, as did the Euro-Americans who often displaced them. Rather, preconquest Indian cultures from coast to coast viewed themselves as part of the natural world in which they lived. They recognized the interplay of natural forces and human behaviors. They saw themselves as part of the whole and acted for the good of the land and its inhabitants, fostering an ecological consensus we seek to recapture in our times.

Dishonor and betrayal were prevalent, too, as they are in any human society. Among the Plains Indians as well as other Native peoples, corrupt acts were redressed through

the decision-making skills of wise leaders. And wise, successful leadership required power and focus—attributes honed
by Cougar Woman.

From childhood on, this outstanding individual lived her
spiritual values, stood by her truth, and attempted to make
life better for her people. Like many women today, she followed her own bright light of inner guidance. Unlike women
of today, she lived in a world of limited opportunities.

More than a century has gone by since this fictionalized
chief rode the lands now known as Yellowstone. New calls for
women leaders are currently resounding in medicine, law,
politics, and international relations. May they, too, be
answered by those with the power and focus to succeed.

In conclusion, I would like to thank my friend, the talent-
ed artist Dee Lambert. Her wonderful cover art and her support are truly appreciated. I would also like to acknowledge
the gifted team that assisted in this launch of *Cougar Woman*—
Ellen Kleiner, for her editorial expertise, which is monumen-
tal, and for her patience with my early morning communica-
tions after she stayed up all night working; Richard Harris,
for his magic in typography and page composition; and
Janice St. Marie, for creatively designing our new look. It is
smashing . . . thank you all.

                                        Jane E. Hartman

Introduction

THE IDEA OF AN AMERICAN INDIAN WOMAN WARRIOR AND CHIEF may come as a surprise. Yet the truth is that some Indian groups had woman leaders. The matrons of the Iroquois, for example, controlled the appointments of the sachems who were to govern. These women were also responsible for throwing the chiefs out if they failed to fulfill their duties. In addition, a number of "squa sachems" were known to exist in New England. These women led their warriors against white invaders as well as Indian foes.

In most Indian nations of the 19th century, women were equal partners in the struggle to survive. They often controlled the wealth and property as well. We "new" Americans, however, have been conditioned to believe that Indian women were submissive and slavelike. This perception appears to have its origins in Europe, where for centuries women had few rights. There it was a white man's world.

I first came across a reference to a Plains Indian woman warrior in 1973 while researching North American tribes for a textbook I was writing. I was fascinated. The Plains cultures were immersed in a hunting and nomadic existence composed largely of counting coups, fighting, and following the bison herds. It was remarkable to find among them a woman who rode as a warrior and who accomplished all the dangerous feats necessary to be hailed as a war leader. The idea lent itself to an action novel about that period in Plains history, decades before the "white flood" engulfed the people and their lands.

To flesh out this story, I have taken a few artistic liberties with history and tribal cultural patterns. My intent was not to misrepresent, but merely to "fill in the blanks" in an attempt to show how a special woman may have lived—an account set forth with an honest heart and great respect for all that was truly Indian.

Historically, the girl was born into the Gros Ventre tribe and adopted by the Absaroke, or Crow, nation. Little appears to have been written about her. Indians did not write history books; nor did non-Indian historians accurately portray Indians until quite recently. As the following words, attributed to Yellow Wolf, a Nez Percé, suggest:

The whites told only one side. Told it to please themselves. Told much that is not true. Only his best deeds, only the worst deeds of the Indian, has the white man told.

No wonder the exploits of one Plains Indian woman were ignored.

Part I

I

Capture

As the war party reached the crest of the hill, Tall Bull saw movement on the plain in front of them. He raised his hand, causing the other six to stop. While the small horse herd with them milled around in confusion, Tall Bull watched, squinting his eyes against the glare. He could make out a light-colored pony with a small rider. Nothing else seemed to be stirring except a herd of antelope and a wind that fluttered the hawk and eagle feathers in his long black hair and waved the grasses like water on a mountain lake.

He urged his horse down the hill with the others close behind. Then, motioning them to continue their route to the mountains, he took off after the stranger.

Tall Bull dug his bare knees into the pony's flanks and leaned forward as the animal responded with a ground-covering run. He liked this spotted horse. It had served him well since he had stolen it from a Nez Percé chief over the mountains. The tribe was famous for its war horses.

Glancing back, he could see the others driving the captured horse herd toward the foothills. They had come a long way. It had been months since they had left their village and gone to raid their lifelong enemies, the Dakotah. They had done well. There were eighteen good horses, many scalps, and he, Tall Bull, had counted coup four times. The Dakotah had stopped chasing them days ago, so their way back to the Absaroke village was an easy one.

He was getting much closer to the rider and could see that the pony was showing signs of fatigue. Tall Bull looked sharply, trying to figure out what kind of Indian it was. Dakotah, he guessed, but something didn't look right. Long black hair flew in the wind as the rider clung to the dun-colored pony's mane. He seemed small and slight, but no matter—another scalp and horse would be welcome.

The fleeing rider turned to look in his direction, and Tall Bull realized with a start it was a young female. He drew alongside his captive, caught her in a vicelike grip, and flung her over in front of him. Then he pulled his well-trained horse to a stop.

For a moment he wondered if he should kill her. Her big dark eyes were defiant. She showed no sign of fear, and she couldn't have been more than ten years old. Half starved, too, he thought.

"Where are you from?" he asked.

She turned her head away in silence.

He pulled his knife and she trembled all over. Then the thought of his woman, Raven, flashed through his mind. She had mourned so at the loss of their only child. Perhaps she would welcome this one. Putting his knife back into his belt, Tall Bull reached out and picked up the rope of her grazing pony. Leading it, he started toward the mountains to join the war party.

The girl remained quiet, but he would not relax his guard. He was too seasoned a warrior for that. He'd seen enemy children plunge knives into their captors before. This girl could ride, though. Almost as well as he did. A smile played around the corners of his mouth, and the many lines webbing the edges of his dark eyes crinkled. She'd given him a run for it. Probably she was wondering what he was going to do to her and where he was taking her. The song of a meadowlark near-by pleased him, but he kept a scowl on his face to scare her.

Without relaxing his vigilance, Tall Bull stopped again just before reaching the top of a rise. He saw no signs of people except where the dust from the herd with the war party showed him their position. Soon they would reach Otter Creek and the mountains. There they would be in Absaroke country and safe, unless they met an enemy looking for hors-es. They would camp tonight, he was sure.

Tall Bull rode into the camp late that night. He found them all asleep around the embers of a fire. The guard near the horses was also asleep. Tall Bull was in the center of the group before they knew it.

"Fools," he shouted at them, "taking your safety for granted. I, like an enemy, could have murdered you."

Tall Bull placed new guards and told one to watch his cap-tive while he slept. After the long ride he was tired and eager to get back to Raven.

Like many warriors, Tall Bull had kept more than one woman—a practice that was economic as well as pleasurable. When a man hunted buffalo, one woman could not keep up with all there was to do. Unlike many, however, Tall Bull had gotten rid of his other women and now had only Raven. She saw to his needs and he was satisfied that it should be so. He fell asleep thinking about her softness.

In the morning the war party mounted early, eager to be on their way. Tall Bull saw that the girl was fed and then put on her horse, but he kept the rope in his hand in case she decided to run. Remembering how she stuck to her horse, he smiled. She was able to handle a horse as well as any youth he had seen. Tall Bull smiled again. Soon he would be able to train the boys in the village to be warriors. He enjoyed his role as teacher. He liked seeing the boys learn to shoot their arrows accurately, although it was getting harder for him to get up before dawn and take them to the icy river for a swim.

He looked back at the girl. Her face was impassive, but her eyes were alert. She was sitting like she was in a daze, her horse picking its way over the loose shale on the path along the creek. Tall Bull wondered what Raven would think of her. He had gotten Raven in much the same way.

It seemed years ago. He had been in Pecunie, or Blackfoot, country stealing horses when he'd seen Raven for the first time. She was getting water from the stream near where he'd been lying in the willows waiting for a chance to steal the black horse tied in front of the chief's tepee. It was a fine horse—a racer if ever he'd seen one. Raven came right past him. He scarcely breathed. He noticed her slimness and how her long hair glistened and her buckskin dress clung to her lithe figure as she bent over to fill the water bags. He didn't dare move a muscle or breathe for fear of being caught. He was so close to her he could have touched her. He ached to do so but did not want the whole tribe after him.

She was beautiful, and he'd give his entire herd of horses for her. That, of course, was impossible, because the Absaroke and the Pecunies were deadly enemies. There was no way for him to get this woman short of stealing her. Tall Bull stopped thinking about it. It was too risky, and besides she might hate him, which he knew he didn't want. From her clothes he could tell she was important. When she went back, he watched her approach the tepee with the black horse. Soon an old warrior came out of the tepee. Tall Bull knew he was a chief. The chief said something to the woman and smiled. As she smiled back, Tall Bull felt his throat tighten. If only she would smile like that at me, he thought, wanting her even more.

That was the beginning. Tall Bull stole the black horse and rode it home. He won several races with it. But he could not forget the Pecunie woman. In his mind she rode beside him everywhere he went. Other women ceased to interest him. Knowing he had to have her or die, he set out to kidnap her, but not until he made several trips to the Pecunie camp to secretly watch her.

Tall Bull's medicine was very strong. He had stolen lots of horses, although he had tried not to steal many from the same tribe at once for fear of arousing their suspicion. Then one day, he knew from a dream that the time had come.

He asked some of his military society, the Foxes, to go with him. "Steal their entire herd," he said. "All I want is the woman."

They agreed and set out on their fastest horses. Tall Bull led the Pecunie horse. He would leave the black in exchange for the girl.

Everything went well. His medicine was working: the hawk feathers in his hair as well as the medicine bundle tied to his waist. He deployed most of the warriors to the other side of the village, telling them to wait until nightfall. With his brother, Elk Heart, he hid in the willows lining the path to the stream and waited. If she did not come today, he would go in and steal her while the others took the herd.

She came late in the afternoon. Tall Bull grabbed her, putting his hand over her mouth and pinning her arms behind her. Elk Heart helped put her on a horse and Tall Bull sprang up behind her. Elk Heart led them into the clear, and they raced the whole night. Tall Bull had his hands full holding her, but the scratches and bruises she gave him didn't bother him.

Memories of his early days taming Raven lulled him into a pleasurable daze. Suddenly the lead of his captive's pony burned through the palm of his hand. Startled, he wheeled his horse around to chase her.

She urged her horse into the swiftly moving stream. Tall Bull galloped to a crossing where he could get over more easily. He could see her horse struggling in the shallows. Tall Bull raced into the river.

She looked as though she would give up without a fight, but he knew she'd try to escape again later. This girl had spirit. Her black eyes looked boldly at him, though she didn't make a sound. Tall Bull wondered what language she spoke, if she spoke at all. Raven, he knew, would find out.

The Absaroke village was nestled in a green valley surrounded by high peaks. A large stream ran through the center of the parkland, giving a plentiful water supply to the thousand head of horses as well as the Indian occupants. Game was abundant here and during the warm months the people had lots to eat.

The village had moved to the high country after the spring hunt. In fall they would return to the buffalo herds of the plains to lay in enough meat for the harsh winter.

The move to the summer grounds had come after the departure of Tall Bull and his war party—all members of the Fox Society. When the villagers broke camp, they placed rocks around the old site and constructed a special pile of rocks to show the direction they were taking.

It was easy for Tall Bull to locate them anyway. He knew of the high valley and followed the Elk River until it met the Buffalo. Its clear glacier-fed waters ran through the valley that had been, for as long as he could remember, the summering place of his tribe.

The war party stopped on a small bluff overlooking the valley. There they put on new moccasins and leggings they had saved for this occasion. Tall Bull wore a handsome pair of leggings that Raven made for him. They were tanned almost white and were very soft. His new moccasins were decorated with colored porcupine quills. He even decorated his horse with eagle feathers in its mane and tail. Then, adjusting his hawk feather headdress that was part of his hawk medicine, he joined the rest of the war party as they raced toward the village.

"EEyaa," he yelled. "Let us show how victorious warriors come home!"

Shouting and brandishing their bows, the warriors drove the captured horses through the village. Tall Bull brought up the rear, leading his captive. The warriors waved scalps, and women ran up to try to take them away. Everyone came out to cheer. Tall Bull looked for Raven. When he saw her standing in front of the tepee, he felt the stirrings of desire for her. How beautiful she was even after many winters. He rode over and handed her the reins of the captured one's horse. Pointing to the girl, he said, "She is for you." Enjoying the pleasure in her eyes, he raced off to join the melee.

That night the women would dance until dawn, and there would be feasting and laughter. Everything was well. Life was happy. Tonight Tall Bull would be with Raven again.

The captured girl looked around the Absaroke camp. Tepees, dogs, children, and adults were welcoming the war party back. She remembered this kind of gaiety from her childhood among her own people. That seemed so long ago. All she could recall in detail was being kidnapped by the hated Dakotah and taken to their camp in the hills black with trees. They had treated her well since they liked children, but she couldn't forgive them for killing her mother. Her mother had tried to stab the warrior taking her child, but it did no good. He took the knife and slit her throat. The girl could still see the pools of blood trailing after her mother as she was dragged away.

She felt tears welling up in her eyes as she pictured it. She dug her fingernails into her hands, wincing from the pain. She could not afford to cry. She was not home, although the shining mountains around her were more like what she remembered.

She looked at the woman holding her horse. The woman's gaze was on the big warrior who captured her. He was kind, she thought. He could have killed her. The tall woman, although no longer young, was pretty. Seeing the woman motion to her, the captured one slid off her horse and stood waiting. The woman pointed to the tepee.

The captured one went into its comfortable interior. In the center a fire was smoldering, giving off heat in the brisk evening air. The floor was covered with buffalo robes and many furs. Various implements of living and warfare decorated the hide walls. She sank down on a soft pile of skins as the woman brought her a bowl of something warm. It tasted good. She was hungrier than she thought. The woman went out, dropping the flap of the tepee and leaving her alone. Suddenly her body felt so heavy she couldn't lift her head. She curled up in the warm nest and went to sleep, oblivious to the sounds of merriment going on in the excited village outside.

Hours later she heard footsteps in the darkness of the tepee. She was then aware of grunts and groans coming from somewhere beside her. Feeling lonely and in need of comfort, she bit her lower lip. As tears welled up in her eyes, she buried her head to avoid hearing the sounds. She was soon asleep again and did not know anything else until morning, when she woke to the sizzle and smell of something broiling.

Sitting up, she discovered the woman bending over the fire. Lying nearby was a huge form covered by buffalo robes. She guessed it was the warrior who had captured her. This must be his tepee and his woman, she thought. Hanging from a pole above her head was a decorated medicine bag. She looked at the fine buckskin. Over it hung the warrior's hawk-feather headdress. The woman saw she was awake and gestured for her to get something to eat. Taking a piece of meat, she began to tear at it with her teeth, the juices running down her chin and onto her crossed knees. She was enjoying it thoroughly when Tall Bull sat up and looked over at her. He said something to the woman and they both laughed. She wanted to laugh too, but was afraid.

The captured one continued to enjoy her meat, wondering what language they spoke. The woman got up and said some words to her. Then the woman said more words, this time in her own language. The captured one nodded and answered. "I am Blackfoot from the high mountains where snow covers the land much of the time."

The woman came over to her and smiled. "I am of the same blood." She patted her head affectionately. "But now I am here and I am happy. You will be happy here also. We live in the tepee of a great man, Tall Bull—a man with very powerful medicine. Tell us how you came to be alone on the plains."

The captured one told the story of how she had been kidnapped by the Dakotah, how her mother had been killed, and how she'd stolen a horse and escaped while the villagers were following the buffalo. She told of evading the military society members who patrolled the fringes of the camp and how she'd ridden in coulees and followed streambeds until she was well away. She'd been riding toward the high mountain peaks trying to find her way home, when she was chased by the warrior who captured her.

The woman repeated the girl's story to Tall Bull, who sat wrapped in a buffalo robe against the chill of the morning. He nodded his head in understanding. "I hate the Dakotah too," he said. "They are always trying to steal Absaroke territory and our plentiful game."

Tall Bull smiled when he heard that the captured one was of the same blood as Raven. No wonder she was so exceptional, he thought. He had not gotten over the way the girl handled her horse. He must see that she had several of her own to train and ride. If he had had a son, he could not have wished for a better rider.

Tall Bull pointed at her. "We shall call you Captured One
Who Rides Like the Wind," he said.

There was no question of her going back to the Pecunies.
He hoped she would be happy. Perhaps he and Raven would
adopt her. It had been done many times. The girl and Raven
were carrying on a long conversation. Tall Bull was pleased.

Summer was a busy time. Women went out in groups and
gathered ripe berries. Old men sat and smoked in the warm
sun, watching youngsters at play and the general activities in
camp. Often, the honored men would sit together on a hillside where they could look down on the village and discuss
tribal matters. Young men hunted, bringing in deer, elk, and
other game. The hides were treated and tanned soft and
almost white. No other tribe could duplicate this process. The
women knew the secret and spent hours making the soft sup-
ple skins for clothes that would be comfortable in the changing weather of the mountains.

This was also a time for lessons. Youths had to learn to be
hard, to fight, and to die. Outstanding feats of valor were the
way to a new name, chiefdom, and popularity.

Tall Bull was a teacher partly by choice, but also because
of his reputation. Before dawn he'd signal all the youths in
his tutelage to meet him at the riverbank. There they would
strip naked and plunge into the freezing water. Great control
was needed to get out of a warm robe and swim in icy water.
It was good to do things that demanded toughness. That
way, one got used to deprivation, to living with very little if
need be.

Tall Bull also took the boys out on rides and conducted
warlike games to show them how to be adept at skills they
would need as warriors. He taught them how to shoot their
arrows accurately, and he rewarded them when they excelled.

When Captured One showed an interest in his own

bone bow and arrows, he decided to teach her too. He also let her care for his horses. He had several that he prized for speed, others for endurance. His best horse could race a buffalo for hours and turn sharply to avoid plunging horns. Captured One took his horses out, exercised them, and kept their coats shining.

One day Tall Bull gave her a black and white pony of her own. Medicine Horse, she called it. That night she had a dream in which she rode Medicine Horse to the top of a mountain and looked down on the whole world. Raven helped her with the words as she told Tall Bull about it. He advised her to remember her dreams, and he was pleased she was learning the language of his people.

When Tall Bull and Raven were sure Captured One showed no wish to run away, they had the criers run through camp telling everyone that she was formally adopted as their own. She was grateful for this act of kindness. And when Tall Bull allowed her to join the boys as he showed them how to use their bows, she was overjoyed. She had played with Tall Bull's bow in the tepee while he was out. It was so heavy she could not pull it.

"I will learn to shoot as well as anyone," she said aloud one day. By now her thoughts of returning to her own people were fading. Her mother was dead. Her father was probably dead too. Warrior deaths were always high unless one's medicine was very potent. Here she had a good home with well-respected people. Raven was of her own blood; Tall Bull was a wealthy man with over one hundred head in his herd, a war chief with powerful medicine. She would learn all he could teach her.

The first morning she joined Tall Bull, they started out at dawn. They went together to the herd and picked two horses. Then they rode around behind the sleeping village and came out on a small hill. Looking down on the camp, they saw tiny spirals of steam and smoke rising from the tepees in the cold morning air. Captured One heard a rustle, and a boy called Small Eagle—the son of Tall Bull's brother—joined them. Then four other boys appeared. Tall Bull looked them over, wheeled his horse, and galloped down the hill. They all followed at top speed. He did not stop until they were in an open glade several miles from camp.

Tall Bull dismounted and took a bundle he had brought from his lodge. He unrolled it on the ground while the youngsters watched.

Then he took out a small hoop and several arrows. He rolled the hoop on the ground, and as it bounced along on the uneven grass, Tall Bull fast as lightning whipped his bow off his back and shot an arrow through the bounding hoop. It stuck in the ground, quivering. The hoop caught on the arrow's shaft, dropped on the grass, and lay still.

Small Eagle retrieved the hoop and arrow. The others lined up with their bows. Tall Bull motioned to Captured One and from his bundle he took out a fine small bow shaped like his own, but of cedar wood and much lighter. He handed it to her, saying, "See if you can shoot as well as you ride."

A boy called Running Fox looked at her with distaste. "Girls ought to stay home in the tepee. They do not belong with men." His eyes were mean and cold.

Captured One ignored him and concentrated on her bow. She imitated Tall Bull, bending her arm back and keeping her elbow slightly flexed as she sighted down the shaft of the arrow. She picked a stump yards away to aim at, but she did not release her arrow.

Tall Bull directed Small Eagle to come to him. The boy did as he was told and stood proudly, careful to do exactly as Tall Bull told him. When he released his arrow, it went close to the hoop target the warrior had set up.

Next Running Fox was called. He was haughty and let his arrow fly too soon. He knew all about shooting. He'd done it by himself and saw no reason to wait for Tall Bull's instructions.

Then a quiet lad called Dreaming Boy—because he was always off by himself daydreaming—went up to Tall Bull. He was not as coordinated as the others, but he worked hard and was in awe of Tall Bull. His arrow dropped off the bow. A second time, he managed to get it airborne.

Finally, Tall Bull called Captured One. Her arrow almost struck the rim of the hoop. Tall Bull was pleased and his eyes twinkled, although otherwise his face remained expressionless. She was glad she had not disgraced him. She treasured the bow he had made for her and would practice until she, too, could send an arrow flying through the eye of the rolling hoop. Small Eagle and the other boys, with the exception of Running Fox, cheered at her success. They would accept her as long as she could hold her own.

But Captured One felt sorry for Dreaming Boy. He was so awkward and he tried hard to be as agile as Small Eagle and the others. She was sure he'd be killed in his first fight. It was too bad he had to be a warrior.

As they rode home after several hours of practice and an icy dip in the Buffalo, Dreaming Boy began to sing in a high-pitched, flutelike voice. First he sang to the water, then to the sun and the birds that flew high in the sky. Captured One, following on Medicine Horse, found herself thinking he had a nice voice—far nicer than that of Running Fox, whose voice was changing and sounded like the croak of a frog. He was slender, too; not so heavily built as the others. He was also nice to her. He had no angry feelings about women learning to shoot.

As the months went by, Captured One became fluent in the language and ways of the Absaroke. She also became skilled with her small bow. Sometimes she would go out on Medicine Horse, taking her bow and arrows in a hide quiver she had stitched with Raven's help, to look for rabbits or other

small game. At times some of the boys would go along. They'd
stalk game, pretending they were sneaking up on enemies. But
her preference was to go alone. Then she would ask the cougar
for its strength and cunning, or the coyote for its canniness, and
she would move so quietly through the scrub that she surprised
grouse and rabbits.

One day she came upon Dreaming Boy sitting on a rock by
a small stream that tumbled down from the high peaks. He
turned languidly in her direction. "I have been looking for the
spirits of the stream," he said. "You can hear them talking if you
listen closely."

Captured One listened, but all she could hear was the patter
of water on rocks. He must be favored if he can hear spirits, she
thought. "What do they tell you?" she asked.

He put his hands in his lap, closed his eyes, and listened.
"They say that you will be a great warrior but that you will not
live a long life. Someone will betray you."

Dreaming Boy opened his eyes, looked at her intensely, and
smiled. "They tell me lots of things. They are often right. Be
careful, Captured One. You will have many enemies before you
travel to the other world."

In the years that followed, Captured One saw a lot of Small
Eagle because he was the son of Elk Heart, Tall Bull's brother.
Often Elk Heart's women set up their lodge next to Tall Bull's,
and there was much coming and going between them. Small
Eagle's mother was not among them, however, for she, like
Captured One's mother, was dead. Small Eagle's greatest joy
was to spend hours at a time with Captured One. Together they
hunted, swam, or spoke about the medicine they would have
when they were older.

Captured One also spent hours sharpening and practicing
with her knife. Finely balanced with a bone handle she'd made
from an elk antler, the knife represented her strength in a man's
world. She learned to throw it as accurately as she used her bow.

Small Eagle knew how good she was with the knife, although he himself did not spend much time knife-throwing, because he was a sturdy boy who would turn into a powerful man. In hand-to-hand combat, Small Eagle would hold his own. Captured One knew that in encounters with naturally stronger foes, she would have to rely on cunning as well as skill in weaponry.

One of the exercises Tall Bull demanded of his pupils was mock horse-stealing. Captured One and Small Eagle often teamed up to practice. Creeping up on a lodge and waiting until no one was about, they'd untie a horse tethered nearby and run away with it. One time Small Eagle caught his foot in a tepee thong and tripped. The warrior in the tepee rushed out with a stick and beat Small Eagle.

Captured One, leading the stolen horse, heard his cries. She ran down the warrior and, helping Small Eagle up behind her, galloped away, leaving the fuming horse owner shouting at them.

Tall Bull praised them for their daring but went no further, giving them the feeling that he didn't approve of their running down a tribesman. It was a good exploit, however, and one that caused Small Eagle to be her most loyal friend.

One of their best adventures gave Small Eagle a new name. All his life he had been in awe of eagles. Once, when he was a baby, a golden eagle landed near his mother's tepee. The great bird stood there looking at him. His mother and father were frightened and drove the eagle off. After that he was called Small Eagle.

He told Captured One that he wanted to take an eagle captive to keep as medicine. How he was going to control the giant bird, much less catch it, was a mystery, but he told her he would dream it first.

Several weeks later he came to Captured One and said: "I know how to get my eagle now. You must help me."

She agreed, and the two of them set off together.

After two hours they rode out into a broad valley surrounded by high mountains. They both knew there were eagles
nesting on the cliffs leading to the heights. Small Eagle pulled
up his pony and pointed to a large flat rock. "This is the place I
saw in my dream," he said. "We shall catch the eagle here, but
first we must dig a pit."

It took several hours to dig a pit deep enough for Small
Eagle to stand up in. They gathered grass and sticks to make a
trapdoor over the pit. When they had finished camouflaging it,
Small Eagle said, "Next we must kill a rabbit."

This took another hour but was accomplished when
Captured One flushed one and put an arrow through its neck.

"Now," Small Eagle said, looking at Captured One as she
brought in the rabbit, "you go behind that big rock with the
horses while we wait. I'll get into the pit, and when the eagle
comes for our rabbit, I'll grab its feet. Then you help me get it
tied up and on my horse."

"You're crazy. That bird will claw you to pieces."

"No, it won't—not after I get its feet caught and tied.
You'll see."

"What about its beak? It can tear meat off bones."

"Maybe so, but I'll put a hood on its head so it can't see."

"All right. You seem to know what you're doing. It's your
medicine and I hope it works. You'll need all the help you can
get." With that, she went behind the rock and settled down to
wait. Several eagles were flying around, but whether any of
them would take the bait was questionable. She hoped they
wouldn't, because she was sure Small Eagle, who really wasn't
small anymore, would get clawed.

Soon one of the big golden birds began circling above the
"hide." Captured One held her breath. The eagle wheeled over
the rabbit, coming closer with each circle. Captured One saw its
head turn to look at the rabbit. The bird swooped in to get its
prey. There was a rush of huge wings as it landed.

Just as the bird tried to carry away its meal, Small Eagle

reached up and grabbed its legs. The eagle screamed in surprise, but he held on to the mighty bird as it beat its wings, furiously trying to get away. Captured One ran to help and threw a small skin over the bird's head.

Small Eagle yelled, "Tie the corners of the skin together so it can't see. Bind its legs. I have a bad cut on my arm and I can't hold on much longer."

Captured One tied the ends of the skin, then whipped thongs around the huge legs of the eagle. Soon it quieted down, and Small Eagle climbed out of the pit. He picked the bird up, adjusting the makeshift hood so the bird could breathe. His arms streamed blood—the eagle had clawed him to the bone.

"Here, wrap these around your arms," Captured One said, handing him a pair of leggings.

The wrappings helped stop the flow of blood and the two of them started back to the village with their prize.

"What are you going to do with the eagle?" she asked.

"I shall tame it and use it as a war eagle. It will go with me when I raid the Dakotah. It can fly ahead and tell me where my enemies are. It will give me second sight."

"It will be your medicine then?"

"Perhaps, if I dream it. I am already named after the eagle and am favored by the golden birds."

"Your arms do not look favored to me. You better let Raven put salve on those cuts." The blood was beginning to seep through the buckskin bandages, and Small Eagle was feeling weak.

They rode into camp carrying the golden eagle and went straight to Captured One's tepee. Tall Bull came out smiling broadly. "You have captured a great bird," he said. "It was a bold move. We shall call you Bold Eagle from now on."

The boy beamed with pleasure. Then, weakened from the loss of blood, he slid off his horse into the arms of Tall Bull. The eagle flopped to the ground and struggled until Captured One caught it.

Hearing the commotion, Elk Heart came over. He was proud of his son and said he would take the eagle and tether it behind his tepee for safekeeping. Captured One was glad to be rid of the straining bird.

She followed Tall Bull into the tepee, where he laid Bold Eagle on the robes. Raven came in, and they both stripped off the leggings covering his arms. There were several deep gashes where the eagle's razor-sharp talons had raked him. Raven bathed them and applied a salve.

Tall Bull looked at the boy. "He has earned the name of a man," he said. "His scars shall prove it."

Captured One wondered how she could earn the name of a warrior. She had to have a powerful dream; eagle-catching was not her way, she knew that. She wished the huge bird could be free again.

Bold Eagle's exploit was told by the criers around camp, and everyone was proud of his bravery. Captured One was admired too, for she had helped the boy in his feat of valor become a man.

The next afternoon Bold Eagle and Captured One were working with the bird when Dreaming Boy came up to them. He was a little afraid of the eagle, whose sharp eyes lanced anything that moved.

"She is a beautiful bird, Bold Eagle. She doesn't like to be a captive, though. I can see it in her eyes."

"No one likes to be a captive. Why should she who likes to fly over the peaks of the world?" Bold Eagle made it clear he had no time for idle conversation. He had important work to do.

"Let him talk, Bold Eagle," said Captured One. "What does she tell you, Dreaming Boy?"

"She says that if you let her be free she will be your medicine and help you as you want, but if you keep her she will betray you. She has babies on the cliff and they will starve if you do not release her."

Dreaming Boy put his hand out to the eagle. She touched it with her beak but did not attempt to bite him.

"Look at that, Bold Eagle. She spends her time trying to bite you, but she won't bite him. She must be talking to him." Captured One was not about to go against what Dreaming Boy had said. She knew he received special messages.

Bold Eagle was taken aback. Every time he went near the eagle, she slashed at him. Maybe there was something in what Dreaming Boy said. "Are you sure of what you say?" he asked.

"I am sure, Bold Eagle. You will have scars to remember her by, but you will have her help if you set her free. Let her go. She's been gone two days and must return to her nestlings."

"Let her go," Captured One repeated. "Dreaming Boy has been right before. If he is wrong, you can catch another eagle."

Bold Eagle was afraid. Dreaming Boy was strange. Everyone knew he had dealings with the spirit world. "All right. Take her tether off, Dreaming Boy. She won't bite you."

Dreaming Boy set the eagle free. For a moment she was motionless, then she lifted into the air with her great wings. They felt the wind in their faces as she flew.

"She will remember her promise to you, Bold Eagle," said Dreaming Boy. "Only men forget their promises."

Just then Running Fox came racing over, out of breath with excitement. "Have you seen the strange man who has come to the village? He is at the chief's tepee. His skin is white. We are going to see the gifts he brought." After speaking, he ran off toward the main chief's tepee in the heart of the village.

A black horse was tethered outside the tepee, and beside it a smaller horse with long ears and packs on its back. The three youngsters, following Running Fox, pushed through the gathering crowd and stared at the strange man sitting on the ground with Weasel Bear, who was passing the pipe. Tall Bull was there and Elk Heart and Hunts-to-Live, each of whom began puffing in turn.

In front of the stranger was a pile of goods. There were odd-looking containers that caught the sunlight and sparkled back like a hundred small suns. The stranger had a long black stick. Pointing at it, Dreaming Boy said, "I've heard of those. They puff smoke and make a bad noise to frighten the game." He moved closer to get a better look.

There were other things in the pile, but the youngsters were not close enough to see them clearly. There seemed to be some kind of cloth or covering with bright colors all over it. The vermilion one was pleasing to them all. There were many more shining containers of all sizes.

The man had a lot of hair on his face. They thought he must be called "Black Hairy Face," because black hair covered most of his cheeks and chin. He was dressed in buckskin like many Indian men, and wore a pair of beaded moccasins. On his head he had a fox skin that covered his hair. He talked rapidly in a deep voice and gestured with his hands.

Pretty soon Weasel Bear got up and went into his tepee. He brought out a fine otter skin and threw it down in front of the stranger. The hairy one gave the chief three of the shiny containers. They were of different sizes and fit together as one. The chief seemed pleased. He pointed to the long black stick, but the hairy one shook his head from side to side.

The bartering went on for several hours with the hairy stranger collecting many skins in exchange for the kettles and other goods. Before too long Dreaming Boy, Bold Eagle, and Captured One were bored and went back to their lodges.

That night when Tall Bull returned to the lodge, he was strangely silent. He seemed to be thinking about something important. After the meal the three of them sat around the fire while Tall Bull smoked his pipe and gazed into the flames.

"Bad things are coming to our people," he said, blowing smoke toward the fire and watching it drift upward. "I don't know how soon, or if we can do anything to prevent it, but I see white people as thick as the buffalo coming into our lands and killing our game. It is in the flames. It must be in the mind of The One Above Who Made All Things. The hairy man who came today is just the first of many. He wanted our furs. Weasel Bear gave him some, but he is not satisfied. I once heard from a Dakotah captive about these whites. They are never satisfied; they want it all. For years we have held on to our country and protected it from our enemies. Now the whites will come and see what beautiful country we have."

Captured One sat in silence. Tall Bull seemed to be talking to himself.

Raven was listening without any expression. She was accustomed to Tall Bull's ways before the fire. He saw ahead of other people and was considered a medicine man. Tonight he spoke bitterly, which made her shudder. She would be glad when the white man went away. Elk Heart, who had three wives and didn't care for any of them, had offered him a woman for the night and he had accepted. He was probably somewhere with her now. Raven supposed the white man had the same wants as all men. She would find out from Elk Heart's woman in the morning. She was glad Tall Bull did not offer *her*.

The next day when Captured One told Bold Eagle what Tall Bull said, he laughed it off. "What can one white man do?"

"Tall Bull said there would be as many as the buffalo."

"We'll wait and see. Meanwhile I am going to the Mountain of the Cougars to see if I can find a strong medicine."

"We'll go together, Bold Eagle. I have to find my own medicine."

"Perhaps Running Fox and some of the others will go. I'll ask them. It won't be long before we move. The time has almost come to find the herds. Look up on the big mountain—there is snow on the peak."

"Yes, the time is close." She left him sitting on a log near the stream that ran beside the village, and went to find Tall Bull. She needed to get her medicine soon. Ahead of her there was a slight commotion. People were watching something. Captured One ran up to see. The white stranger was riding away leading his packhorse with the load of pelts he'd gotten from Weasel Bear. She spat on the ground. It was good to be rid of him—the air would smell better.

She must ask Tall Bull for his blessing before going to the mountain. She hoped he would approve. Not many girls went on a vision quest, but she was different and she knew it. She felt Tall Bull would not stand in her way. He might even help her with his hawk medicine. She had seen him take it out and meditate over it many times before going on a raid. He often saw visions at these times. But this summer he had not gone out on war parties. Other times, when he did, he ate some of his medicine. She was not sure what it was, but it looked like fine white powder. She knew the hawk feathers he wore behind his ear were part of it too. She also knew it was powerful.

Tall Bull was sitting in front of the lodge in the sun when she got home. She sat beside him and said nothing. They looked across the stream at the green valley surrounded by the craggy mountains. There was a dust of snow on the highest ones. The geese would be flying soon and it would be time to leave. Then the camp would be in a frenzy as all the families moved. She enjoyed the peace and solitude of the high country. Tall Bull's dire predictions about the whites seemed far away. So did their other enemies, although the young men were going off on raids and bringing in horses from time to time. Soon she would go to steal horses. She wanted to have a thousand head of her own.

"Summer is leaving us. I am sad to see it go," Tall Bull said, looking at her fondly. He was beginning to show his age, she thought, with white streaks in his long hair.

"Yes, it is time I went to the mountains and sought out my medicine."

Tall Bull looked surprised, but he was indulgent. He loved this bright-eyed youngster. "You want to go on a vision quest?"

"Yes, father. I need to find a strong medicine."

"There is no reason for you to find your own. I can give you some of mine." He thought to spare her the journey.

"No, I want to find my own. I am different and yours may not work as well for me."

Tall Bull considered this slowly, still savoring the view of the mountains he loved.

"Yes, you are right," he said at last. "You may go." He put his hand out and touched Captured One. "Perhaps you will find a new name to help you. You have many strange gifts. You will do well."

"Thank you, father." She thought of how she would go up into the mountains as soon as Bold Eagle was ready, tomorrow or maybe the next day. Together they would seek their separate medicines. She knew she would be able to find hers. Bold Eagle would have to watch out for himself. She wondered if Dreaming Boy would find a medicine strong enough to protect him. He was no fighter. In fact, he still couldn't hit the target with his arrows. His days would be few if he went to fight. She felt sorry and vowed silently to try to help him. The One Above must look after people like that, she thought.

Raven came around the tepee to join them. She smiled at Tall Bull. "The white man has left," she said. "He took many furs with him and left many goods. Elk Heart's woman gave me one of the kettles. It is small but strong, and will hold water without leaking. I will use it to heat water and cook in."

Tall Bull nodded. He was pleased when she was happy. "It would be well if we do not take the white man's goods. They will make us soft."

Raven began to giggle. She looked lovely when she laughed, thought Captured One. Her whole face lit up and her eyes sparkled. "Elk Heart's wife told me that sleeping with the white man was like being with a rutting buffalo bull. She is bruised all over this morning. She couldn't wait to get into the river and wash herself off. He stank too, she said. I think she is afraid the smell won't come off."

Tall Bull didn't reply. He thought it disgusting of his brother to give the white man one of his wives. He wouldn't want her again himself. But Elk Heart was not involved with women. He kidnapped wives when he wanted a new one—which was often. He was like a buck rabbit, hopping off one and onto another. Unlike his brother, Tall Bull knew he'd kill anyone who tried to take Raven. Most men knew it and left her alone.

As dusk approached, Captured One began to gather together the small bundle she would take with her to the Mountain of the Cougars. She did not need much—her weapons and some clothes and a robe for warmth at night. She might store food along the way, but she would not eat until her medicine had come to her.

2

Vision Quest

Dawn was breaking when the youngsters sneaked out of the village. They were to meet at a prearranged spot across the river.

The War Clubs, a military society that patrolled the village, were not in evidence when Captured One took her horse and silently led it to the riverbank. She waded in leading Medicine Horse. When the icy waters reached her thighs, she began to swim propped up against him, with her left arm over his neck. No sound but the rushing of the current was audible. Once on the other side, she rode the pony through the tangled willows to the meeting place.

Bold Eagle was already there. Seeing her, he raised his arm in welcome. "No one else has come, but we should wait a while longer."

"Maybe they got caught by the War Clubs."

The crackling of a twig alerted them. It was Running Fox with Dreaming Boy. Running Fox looked at Captured One and sneered, saying, "So the brave woman is going to try to have a vision. You will starve or be eaten by a grizzly. You should stay home where women belong."

Captured One ignored him. He was distasteful to her and she did not see anything to be gained by talking back. Some day she would get even with him.

Dreaming Boy was bundled up in a buffalo robe. He looked chilled and pale in the breaking light. He said nothing, but appeared frightened of this excursion to meet with the supernatural even though he had had many such experiences. He was not looking forward to being a warrior or to getting a fighting medicine. He preferred to stay at home and pick berries with the women, or sit and watch the animals that came to the river in great numbers. The bears especially fascinated him as they fished in the waters or ate in the berry patches. Killing did not appeal to him, but he knew that unless he had a very unusual vision, he must follow the war trail.

"Is anyone else coming?" Bold Eagle asked.

The other three seemed to agree no one would follow. They started off cautiously until they were well away from the War Clubs. Then they broke into a brisk canter and headed out of the valley into the hills toward Cougar Peak. They rode in silence for several hours before Bold Eagle pulled up his mount.

"This is where I shall leave my horse," he announced. "I prefer to go on foot to find the place that suits me."

"I will join you for a while until I find the spot I am looking for," Captured One said, turning her horse free to graze.

Dreaming Boy and Running Fox stayed on their horses. They were having a hard time making up their minds.

"We leave you here then and shall return in three days to this spot. We go to find our medicine fathers." Bold Eagle took his small bundle and started up a game trail at a good clip. Captured One followed.

Dreaming Boy remained with his horse while Running Fox turned and galloped away. He disappeared behind some large trees.

"Wait for me," Dreaming Boy yelled after Bold Eagle. He turned his horse loose and, clutching his robe and a spare pair of leggings, trotted after them.

Bold Eagle stopped partway up the trail and took some food from his bundle to put in a hanging cache. "Store any food you have in here. We will eat it when we come down."

Soon they were on their way up the trail, which became steeper as they neared the overshadowing peak. An hour later they were still climbing, following a rushing stream. Berry bushes beside the water were loaded down with luscious-looking red fruit, and they saw many bears.

Before long, they came out on a ledge. The earth was golden from the rising sun to the east.

"I shall stay here," Captured One said, setting down her bundle and spreading out her robe. Bold Eagle and Dreaming Boy went on up the ridge. She didn't think Dreaming Boy would go much farther. Bold Eagle, she knew, would get as close as possible to the eagles' nests up top.

Captured One sat on her robe and looked about her. The high peaks of the mountains all around had traces of snow on them. Down in the valley the river wound sinuously, reminding her of a curved snake. At eye level, she could see eagles and hawks catching the updrafts and gliding on the currents.

She noticed tiny black dots in an open area near the river: a herd of elk or even a small group of buffalo, she thought. There were no great herds of buffalo in the valley, because they stayed out on the endless plains. As far as the eye could see, the plains were black with them, a giant tide that moved restlessly. During the few years that she had been with the Absaroke, she had seen the fall and spring hunts. Until this year she had been too young to do more than help Raven process the killed buffalo. This year would be different. She would kill them herself.

After a while Captured One dozed off, only to be wakened by the cawing of a raven. When she raised her head, she saw the raven looking at her. It hopped up on a rock to get a better view.

"What is the matter with you?" she asked the big black bird. It came closer, still cawing.

"I have nothing to give you," she explained. The bird cocked its head and flew off.

Captured One settled back against a rock and began to think about Tall Bull's medicine. He had told her about it once: "I sat on the mountain for four days before my medicine father came in the form of a hawk. He took me through a deep tunnel that was so dark I was afraid, but soon we came out on the roof of the world. I saw much that would happen to me; I even saw the coming of the white men."

Tall Bull had had many visions, Raven had told her. Raven also seemed to think that Captured One had powers.

She felt hunger gnawing at her stomach. The first day was scarcely over. What will the next one bring? The air was getting chilly, so she gathered her robe around her and huddled against the rock wall. Despite the robe, she was cold and not at all sleepy. Darkness, meanwhile, slowly enveloped the world. A thin moon hung in the far corner of the sky like a small window of light.

She wondered about the world where slain warriors went, where all dead creatures went—humans, buffalo, deer, everything. Perhaps it was spring all the time there, or maybe summer.

The warriors she had known never seemed to fear death. They knew, she decided. Tall Bull knew too. Death was natural to all things. They knew that life was an unending circle. A circle like the moon whose fullness was hidden from her. It would return, as life returns to all things that only appear dead.

As the night wore on, Captured One fell into a sound sleep, but she had no dreams. She awoke at dawn to see the sun coming over the peaks. The world looked fresh and clean.

She sensed something watching her from the rocks. Slowly she turned and saw a tawny cougar sitting above her. It was staring at her, its tail twitching slightly.

Captured One didn't move. She stared at the animal, wondering why it had come. Was she blocking its way down the mountain?

The cougar stood and stretched, then gave a mighty yawn. Captured One blinked her eyes and it was gone.

Her excitement died away and the hunger pangs returned, ferociously attacking her insides. Setting her mind on other things, she thought about the great cougar and how fine it looked, so sleek and strong and quiet. When it killed a deer, she imagined, it did so with one swift stroke.

The day passed slowly for her. That night she slept fitfully, hearing furtive noises and feeling wings touching her face.

The next morning she didn't feel like waking up. Forcing herself to stand and stretch her arms toward the sky, she cried, "Oh One Above, please send someone to show me the way." When she sat down, her head swam and she became nauseous. She began to sing Tall Bull's medicine song to herself. She had heard him sing it many times to the hawk as it flew in the sky. "Hawk," she cried, "help me. Help me like you have helped Tall Bull, my father." Her voice sounded weak and far away. It seemed to be carrying on the breeze and echoing across the valley. "Hawk, hear me—please help me find my medicine father."

Nothing happened. The sun became hot and her mouth felt dry as sand. Her tongue was so parched it felt prickly.

She decided it was time to offer her little finger to the spirits in hopes that they would assist her. Placing her left hand on a stone, she took her knife, squinted her eyes, and chopped off the fingertip. She felt nothing as the blood gushed out on the gravelly ledge. She picked up the tiny fingertip and put it on a high ledge for the spirits. "Help me," she called. "It is for you." Then she lost consciousness.

She was awakened by a voice booming across the sky. *Wake up and look for me. I am here to help you.*

She opened her eyes and looked around. She could see nothing.

Are you searching? The voice came from everywhere.

She stood up, walked to the ledge, and saw a touch of gold above where she had been sitting. It was the cougar.

Do you see me now? The cougar leaped down beside her. *Follow me and I shall show you what you may live to see.*

The cougar took her to a hole in the upper rocks. Its golden tail disappeared into the darkness. Captured One crouched and pulled herself in.

The cave was decorated like the tepee of a chief. There were great buffalo robes on the floor. The walls were covered with skins, yet they twinkled brightly with the light of a thousand small stars, bathing the room in a soft glow.

The cougar had a young cub that came tumbling out to greet them. Captured One petted the small creature as the cougar lay down on a white buffalo robe. *Watch the opening of the cave,* the cougar said.

Suddenly the entrance transformed into a broad grassy plain and, in the middle, a large square house that seemed to be made of tree trunks. At its four corners flew colored birds.

On the outside of the strange dwelling were tepees pitched in rows. She looked at them, trying to make out whose they were. They were not Absaroke, she could see that. Then several riders appeared. They *were* Absaroke; she could tell by their clothes and their proud bearing. One had long flowing hair with eagle feathers in it. Bold Eagle, she thought—except here he was bigger and his shoulders more massive. Next to him was a smaller warrior on a black horse. This warrior had a skin over one shoulder and long hair decorated with a single eagle feather. It was Captured One. Suddenly Bold Eagle slumped forward on his horse. She reached over and, taking his horse's rope, raced into the

opening of the dwelling. Behind them a war party was howling and shooting arrows.

The warriors ran in a circle around the dwelling. Then she
saw herself come racing out. The attackers, Pecunies, scattered. Two of them were lying on the ground and she was
chasing the others away. Captured One sat on the floor of the
cougar's cave feeling weak. Was this really to happen?

*You will be a great chief and lead many successful raids. You will
be the only woman chief your tribe shall ever know. But look, there is
more.*

The scene in front of her changed, and buffalo plains covered the opening. The grass was green and it waved in the
wind. Something about the landscape, however, didn't look
right. Then she realized that there were no buffalo. The plains
were empty.

"Where are the buffalo?" she asked.

Gone. You may not live to see this, but it will happen. Look—

A strange object crossed the empty plains like a snake. It
moved along with great billows of dirty black smoke coming
out of its head. The thing kept going in a straight line.

"What is that?" she asked.

It will carry people inside it.

"What about our people? Where are they?"

*They will be on earth, but they will not do well. Your father has
told you what will happen.*

The scene changed again. Riders dressed in blue filed
across the plains, dark as a stormy sky. They wore broad
head-coverings and rode two by two. There were thousands
of them, riding in an endless line toward the horizon. They
rode up into the mountain valleys, and before them the
Indians fled. Then she saw her people, poor and sick, struggling in the snow.

"Don't show me any more," Captured One said. She sat
with her head in her hands and wept. "I do not want to see
more."

Then let me show you how to get your medicine. The cougar stood beside her. *It will protect you until your time comes. It will make you strong, brave, and wise. Above all, you must be wise, because others will resent you. When the dawn breaks, you will go down the mountain. On the trail you will find marks of a male cougar. Follow these tracks and you will see him waiting for you. Kill him with one arrow through the heart. Take his skin with you wherever you go; also take his heart. These will be your medicine. Sing to me when you need help. You will have the heart, the cunning, and the power of a cougar. Now go.*

Captured One slept until morning and woke up feeling refreshed. Her visit with the cougar seemed like a dream, but she knew it was more than that. Remembering what the animal had told her, she rolled up her robe and started down the trail. Her feet seemed to fly along until she came to the muddy tracks of a huge cougar. They were fresh, and she felt her excitement mount.

Holding her bow and arrow ready, she followed the tracks over some rocks to a small glade. There, lying by a pool, was a big male cougar. He looked at her but made no effort to move. What a beautiful beast, she thought, but he is very old. Remembering her medicine, she asked his forgiveness. "I do not want to kill you," she said, "but you are my medicine and you shall be with me wherever I go. Do not hold this against me. I do only as I have been told by powers greater than myself."

She aimed carefully and shot an arrow through his heart. He slumped over and lay dead.

It took her a while to skin the cougar. Her mutilated finger throbbed painfully. Finally, she rolled up the great skin and took the heart, which she would dry and powder. Then she made her way down the mountain to the food cache. No one else was there, so she ate and rested.

Dreaming Boy was the next to appear. He looked happy, which surprised her. She was pleased to see him, as she had feared he might get into trouble on the mountain alone.

"I had a vision that revealed many strange and wonderful things," he said, sitting beside her and taking some food. "Let me tell you about it." He was very excited.

"When we left you, Bold Eagle went up the mountain, but I took another path and came to a small waterfall. The berries were thick and birds were singing. I thought this was a good place to stay, so I took off my clothes and swam in the water. Later I stretched out on my robe and slept. I didn't dream that night, but the next morning I saw bear tracks all around, showing that bears had walked on my robe and sniffed my body.

"I did not see a bear the entire day; I just sat and contemplated the falling water. I was hungry, but I have fasted before so this did not bother me. That night I went to sleep in the same place, but I woke in the middle of the night. Everything was black—so black I couldn't see a thing, yet I heard the bears breathing all around me. I knew they were sitting in a circle watching me.

"Their chief said to me in a booming voice: *Boy, you will never be a warrior. Tomorrow you will have a dream that will tell you how to live. You will be given powers of second sight as well, to use only for good purposes.*

"Then I heard grunting and growling as the bears in the circle agreed. They got up and shuffled off. I could hear them go.

"The next evening I lay on my robe watching the sky as it grew dark. The night birds were crying, and I heard the voice of a wolf nearby. I waited for the dream that would show me how to live. It came many hours later.

"I heard a voice call my name: *Dreaming Boy, get up and look at me. I am over by the pool.* There in a shining light stood a beautiful woman. She had long black hair flowing to her ankles and was dressed in a white robe with exquisite designs. She stretched out her arms toward me. In one hand she held a berry basket, and in the other a war club. I reached for the club, as I knew I should, but she withdrew it and made me take the basket. She told me: *You will never be a warrior. You will work as a woman and you will see into the future. Your name shall be Sweet Grass. Now take the basket and go down the mountain to your friends. We will meet again and you will hear me singing in the streams."*

He paused in his story and scrutinized Captured One for her reaction. "Does this surprise you?"

"No," she said. "I am glad it happened this way. Come into my lodge, Sweet Grass, and take care of my things, because I shall not have time for women's work."

He considered her offer but did not answer. He wanted to think only about his vision. "Her song was so beautiful. I will never forget it. I have heard it many times in the mountain streams, not knowing what I heard. Tell me about your dream, Captured One."

"A cougar came to me and took me to her cave. It was just like the lodge of a great chief. I saw many things, several of them unhappy. Much of what Tall Bull says about the future will come true and I am very sad. I am to be a chief and the cougar is my medicine." She pointed to the tawny skin rolled up beside her.

"You will be a great chief someday, Captured One."

"I couldn't look at the future any longer—it was too much to take at once. But another time I shall find the cougar again."

Sweet Grass was understanding. Sometimes he wished he did not see so much, though he was glad his visions rarely showed him anything about himself. He knew Captured One had a destiny and he wanted to comfort her.

She changed the subject. "I am worried about Bold Eagle. Do you think we should look for him?"

"Let's try to find him before he is exposed too long."

They started up the mountain trail. The horses picked their way carefully as the trail steepened. Before long they passed the side path to the waterfall where Sweet Grass had had his vision and, just beyond, the trail to Captured One's ledge. Here the main trail narrowed, and above them they could see mountain goats grazing on the meager browse. Still there was no sign of Bold Eagle.

Sweet Grass pointed to dark birds circling high in the air. "Look. If we follow them, we will find Bold Eagle."

The trail was getting more difficult. Captured One jumped down and ran ahead on foot.

The trail ended on a bare rock face in the center of which they saw Bold Eagle's body. He was naked and bloody. Vultures were circling but had not gotten enough nerve to land. When Captured One and Sweet Grass approached, the birds flew farther away. Captured One rolled Bold Eagle over, hoping he was not dead. What had he done to himself? His middle finger was cut off to the second joint and the stump was oozing blood. His body was scratched in a hundred places. She squeezed water on his face. His cheeks twitched in response and his eyes flickered open, but there was no recognition in them.

The two put Bold Eagle on one of the horses and Sweet Grass got up behind him, then they carefully picked their way down the mountain. As they came into the valley, Captured One heard something. She signaled to Sweet Grass and rode into the willows to hide.

"Someone is coming down the trail," she said, fingering her bow and taking an arrow out of her quiver. "We are in no shape to run or to fight."

Soon several riders came down the stream through the trees. Captured One sighed and raced out of hiding to greet Tall Bull. Elk Heart and two other Fox Society members were with him.

Tall Bull lifted Bold Eagle off the horse and laid him down in the shade. He bathed his nephew's wounds, and the others fed him tiny scraps of meat.

"That is the best medicine he can have now," Tall Bull said, covering Bold Eagle with a robe. They all relaxed under the trees and enjoyed some fresh deer meat. As she ate, Captured One reminded herself that she must tell Tall Bull and the other honored men about her vision and have them tell her what it all meant. Sweet Grass must do the same.

Tall Bull was interested in her cougar skin. She opened it up and spread it before him. The other warriors stood looking, and she sensed new respect in them. It was a big animal and an almost perfect skin. She showed Tall Bull the great beast's heart, and asked if he would help her powder it so she could use it as he did his hawk medicine.

Tall Bull was proud of her. "We will change your name after this brave thing. It takes great courage to kill a cougar on its own mountain. What else did you learn?"

She told him about the cougar's cave and her vision of what was to come.

Tall Bull was not surprised. "I, too, have seen the lines of men in blue," he said. "They are white conquerors and they will take our lands. Behind them are thousands of others greedily reaching for what is ours. They shall take it all and leave us nothing. I have not seen the snake on the prairie that you speak of. Where were the white people?"

"They rode inside it, and when it stopped, they spilled out like vomit from its sides. It gave off lots of smoke, turning our blue skies gray and covering the sun."

Tall Bull thought about what she said. It sounded strange, but much of her vision was true to what he had seen, and others before him. She had received powerful medicine from the cougar, and he was pleased. In fact, her name must show that she had the heart of this great beast.

He looked at her and said, "You shall be known as Cougar Woman. The criers shall tell the people about your exploits when we return."

Bold Eagle was stretching. Seeing his friend, he smiled in recognition. "How did I get here?" he asked her.

She told him the story of how she and Sweet Grass, formerly Dreaming Boy, had gone up the mountain to find him nearly dead. "What happened to you, Bold Eagle?" she asked.

"I went to the mountain hoping to see my eagle father, but I saw nothing. As I sat there I heard a big wind rushing around the peaks. There were no eagles to be seen. I decided I must do something to make the spirits feel sorry for me and to evoke their help. I chopped off my finger." Bold Eagle held up his hand with the still bloody finger stump. "It bled like it would never stop," he added.

"Then I got up and started walking, trying to find the eagles that live near the peak. It did me no good. I came into a meadow where bears were picking berries. They chased me through the thickets, and I felt the brambles cut me into a thousand pieces with their tiny knives. Finally I came out onto a flat rock and collapsed. My legs had dissolved.

"I cried to the eagles, but all I saw were black and ugly birds of death circling above me. Before I lost consciousness, I felt their cold eyes on me. But I did not find my spirit helper. It was a wasted trip for me."

"Next time you will find your eagle father," Cougar Woman said. "I know it. But now we shall go home and rest. Later, Sweet Grass and I will tell you about our experiences on the mountain."

Bold Eagle smiled and closed his eyes.

The warriors put him on a pony they had caught downstream. Then they all rode slowly back to the Absaroke village. It had been an exciting few days, she thought. Her cougar medicine gave her all the power she needed to work toward being a chief. Even now she could sense a difference in the way Tall Bull's friends treated her. They were in awe of her powers. Cougar Woman, pleased with herself, sat straighter on her horse.

Tall Bull arranged to have a crier tell the people in the village that Cougar Woman was coming home with her medicine and a new name. A second crier was to announce Sweet Grass's new status as a woman; and a third crier, to give news of Bold Eagle.

By the time the riders arrived in camp, people were in front of their lodges clapping their praise. This was the first time in many generations that a woman had been so honored. It was a great thing and would bring new prosperity and good luck to the people. They were all glad for her and proud to be part of the occasion—except Running Fox.

When Running Fox had left them at the mountain, he had decided not to bother finding his medicine. It was easier to buy it from an old warrior. He would do that instead of making himself uncomfortable. So he returned to the village. If they questioned him, he'd make something up. That was easy enough.

As the criers ran through, he was sitting behind his tepee smoking his father's pipe. He spat in disgust and scorn when he heard the news. The warrior woman did not appeal to him. He liked his women submissive. Besides, she could outshoot and outride him, enjoying it every time she did.

Sweet Grass was abominable too. Was he really to be called Sweet Grass? Stinking Grass would be better. He felt under his loincloth and handled himself lovingly, wondering if Sweet Grass would cut that off too. What was he—a he or a she? That was it; Sweet Grass was to play a woman's role from now on, as his spirit helper had told him. It would be accepted by everyone but him, Running Fox.

And she—a warrior? He grinned nastily, thinking he'd like to catch her alone without her shadow, Bold Eagle. He'd see how strong a warrior she was. Running Fox went back to his smoking, keeping an eye open for his father, who would be furious if he caught his son with his best pipe.

They had not been back long before Cougar Woman decided to try out her new medicine by stealing horses from an enemy. She knew Tall Bull would not agree that she should go so soon, but she was sure Bold Eagle would go with her. Even though he had not had a vision, his eagle medicine was strong enough to protect him on a raid of this sort. Didn't the captured eagle say she'd take care of him?

Cougar Woman told Bold Eagle of her plan and he agreed to go. Late that night, they both sneaked out of camp and rode off toward the buffalo plains, where they hoped to find enemy camps. She had her cougar skin over her shoulder and the powdered heart in a medicine bundle at her waist. She felt well protected, and she knew what awaited them, for Sweet Grass had told her that on the plains they would find four horses tied in front of Dakotah lodges: two black ones were for her, and two brown ones for Bold Eagle.

They rode for hours without stopping. Cougar Woman was on Tall Bull's fastest horse, and Bold Eagle was riding Elk Heart's racer—animals that had to be well taken care of.

They camped overnight and the next day rode hard to the east, following the river until they gradually came into the foothills. As the land flattened and opened up, they saw more and more buffalo. The next day they would be on the plains.

Their first view of the vast sea of buffalo herds made them stop in their tracks. The One Above had put these creatures on earth to take care of his people, and for this they were grateful. Their time-out for gratitude was short-lived, however, for there was action to their left. Running beasts were kicking up dust as riders chased them. Hidden safely behind a clump of trees, the two watched the horsemen kill several buffalo and saw women come to butcher them. After a while Bold Eagle went scouting and came back to report a small camp of ten lodges beside a nearby stream.

That night after the sun went down, Cougar Woman and Bold Eagle sneaked up on the camp. Just as Sweet Grass had predicted, the lodges belonged to the Dakotah and four horses were tied up in front of them. Two were black and the other two brown. They tethered their own horses in a thicket by the stream and crawled up closer to wait until everyone was asleep. Later, finding no guards on the premises,

Cougar Woman and Bold Eagle crept into the heart of the
Dakotah camp.

Cougar Woman paused outside the first tepee and listened.
All she could hear was deep snoring coming from inside. She
approached the first black horse, cut its tether, and walked the
animal slowly to the next one. Cutting the second black horse
free, she led them both out of camp. Then she jumped on one
and, leading the other, galloped to the thicket to meet up with
Bold Eagle.

He had not yet returned. Soon she heard an uproar and
looked up to see him galloping in with the two browns and
pursuers on his trail. They switched to their fast horses and
raced for their lives, driving the captured animals with them.
They did not relax until the second night, when they were sure
they had safely escaped the Dakotah. Cougar Woman looked
at the spotted horse prized by Tall Bull. It was strong and well
trained. It knew what was expected of it. She walked to rest
the horses.

"Perhaps we should switch animals to rest them further,"
Bold Eagle suggested.

"You are right." She stopped and caught one of the new
blacks. It seemed like a good horse, with its sleek ebony
body, white lightning streak down its face, and long tail and
mane.

Bold Eagle got on one of the brown horses and galloped
beside her. "The people will be excited when we come in this
time," he said. "Let's race through the village, driving our new
horses." She nodded.

Just outside camp they mounted their own horses and,
driving the stolen ones, raced through the camp, whooping
and yelling. People came out to see what was going on and
clapped their praise of the two youngsters and their first
coups. Taking a tethered horse from an enemy was one of the
four principal honors needed to become a great warrior and
chief.

Bold Eagle turned to Cougar Woman and said, "It is good. Next we shall go on the war trail, but I must get my eagle medicine first."

Tall Bull and Raven were pleased with the two black horses. Tall Bull told Cougar Woman she had done well. Raven, however, chastised her for running off at night and not waiting until she was older. Secretly Raven hoped that the girl would take an interest in staying home and finding herself a young man, perhaps Bold Eagle.

But Cougar Woman's greatest desire was to go on a war party and find her destiny. As for young men, she had seen Running Fox looking at her from time to time and always ignored him. If he came too close, she'd slit his belly open with her knife. He was meaner than a Dakotah and could not be trusted. She must remember to be on her guard around him. Bold Eagle, however, could be trusted; he was her brother.

That night the villagers celebrated and Cougar Woman recounted how they sneaked into the Dakotah camp and stole the horses. Bold Eagle corroborated her story. They had done well and everyone praised them both. Even Sweet Grass, who had no stomach for war, was proud of their courage. It took a brave warrior to sneak into the enemy's camp. Her cougar medicine was working.

Tall Bull was proud of Cougar Woman. In the fire he saw her future: It followed the war trail.

Several days later Sweet Grass became a member of Tall Bull's lodge. He had assumed the clothing and life of a woman, in keeping with his vision. Tall Bull had given his permission, glad that Raven would have help. In the way of his people, he accepted Sweet Grass's new role and treated him as a woman.

Bold Eagle was determined to get his medicine, and this time he would go alone. One morning before dawn, he sneaked off, rode to the foot of the Mountain of the Cougars, and let his horse loose. The eagle, he hoped, would come to him and sing its song and tell him what he needed to know.

He chose a steep trail made by elk and other game. After climbing for a long time, he came onto a windswept ledge. Before him the mountain went straight up. Aware that he could not possibly reach the peak from here, he stayed where he was. He took off his clothes and, standing naked in the cool wind, cried to the eagles. He could see them as they flew overhead, but they ignored his calls, so he sat down and leaned against the wall of the cliff. He had no robe to lie on, though he did have some leggings and a shirt, which he stretched out on as the hours passed. The eagles that flew by still showed no signs of acknowledging his presence.

Come sunset, the air turned cold and he could see black clouds covering the neighboring slopes as well as the peak above him. It must be snowing on the heights, he thought, dressing as warmly as possible. He shivered through the night, sleeping in snatches. Each time he woke he wondered if he should even be out so late in summer. He knew the camp would soon be moving to lower country to hunt the buffalo for a winter's supply of meat and robes.

The next day was gray and cold. Clouds swallowed the nearby peaks, and although it felt like snow, no flakes fell. He could hear the screams of the eagles, but he could not see them. He sat exposed to the elements.

As evening approached, he fell asleep. In his dream he was on foot in a broad green valley full of antelope, buffalo, and other game. He had to shoulder his way through the herds. The cliffs that rose straight up on either side of him were flaming red. Then he heard a cry. It was an eagle on a cliff ledge calling his name.

Bold Eagle, come up here to me.

He started toward the eagle, climbing up the sheer rock face by using the handholds chinked out of the wall. The eagle continued to call to him, saying, *Keep climbing. You are getting closer.*

At last he came out on a ledge. The bird was beside him. She spread her wings as if to shelter him.

I am your medicine, Bold Eagle. Have faith in me, for I shall lead you to fame. As long as you protect me, I shall protect you. I will give you my eyes to see with forever, and my wings to soar with on the roof of the world. You have a friend, Bold Eagle, who is true to you. Look on her not as a woman but as a great warrior. Together you will do well. When you go to fight, Bold Eagle, sing my song and wear my feathers, which you will find before your return. Now go back to the buffalo plains. You will have a mishap but will be saved from harm.

Bold Eagle woke up shivering and cold as ice. Everything around him was white with thick flakes of snow. He pulled on his leggings and moccasins and started down the trail. It was slippery going, and he slid a good part of the way. But he made it to the bottom quickly. There he killed a rabbit and built a fire under an overhanging rock to cook his prey. After eating the hot meat he felt better, though still cold. As he nestled against the sheltering rock enjoying the warmth of the fire, something scratched at his back. It was an eagle tail feather—fresh looking, as if it had just been plucked. Glancing around, he found four more. He tucked them carefully away in his bundle and settled down to wait for the storm to let up.

At last the snow stopped and the sun began to shine. Bold Eagle threw sand over his fire and, picking up his small bundle, started looking for horse tracks. He found his horse sheltering in a thicket by the stream, and he rode back to camp.

From a small hill behind the village, he saw lodges coming down and families rounding up their herds in preparation for the move to buffalo country. Criers were going through the village calling, "Pack up—we are moving. The chiefs say to get ready. We move to hunt the buffalo."

Bold Eagle raced his horse down the slope and over to his fallen tepee. Elk Heart's women were packing everything up. To each horse rounded up for hauling they were fastening two lodge poles so their ends would drag. On crossbars between the poles they were piling utensils, robes, and other paraphernalia. In the days before horses, he remembered hearing, these handy travois were attached to dogs. Now dogs ran free, except for the more reliable ones used to carry small packs.

He heard a cry from behind. It was Cougar Woman. "I am glad you are back, Bold Eagle. I was going to look for you if you didn't come today. Did you have a dream?"

"Yes, I have good medicine. I will tell you later."

Bold Eagle helped his family pack up their belongings. Then lines began to form. The chiefs and the old men went first. The old men would find a good campsite every night and gather firewood or buffalo chips. These seasoned elders knew where to set up camp.

Tall Bull, because he was a chief, rode in front with the other honored men. The head chief, Weasel Bear, rode at the head of the line, carrying his pipe. Now and then, some of the arrogant young military society members whooped and raced ahead, displaying high spirits and showing off. Bold Eagle and Cougar Woman looked with envy at them, yearning for the day when they would have the privilege of riding in front.

The village was composed of several hundred families, and moving was a slow process. To protect everyone, the military society members rode the periphery, keeping alert for enemies who might seize this vulnerable moment to swoop down and attack. The move would take many days, but by the time they arrived at the selected site near the hunting grounds, the old men would be ready for them and the place prepared. The village was to be set in several circles, each one surrounding the tepee of an honored man.

Bold Eagle and Cougar Woman were excited. This year for the first time, they were old enough to hunt the buffalo.

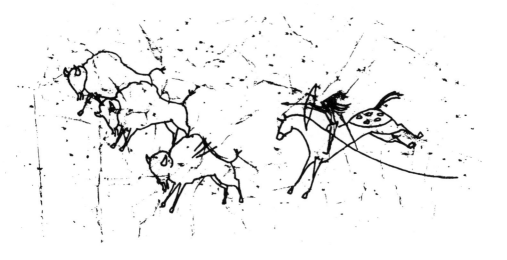

3

Buffalo Hunt

I⟍T TOOK MANY DAYS FOR THE ENTIRE VILLAGE TO REACH THE NEW location. The move was orderly, however, even though the great number of people and animals stretched in a long, noisy, confused-looking line.

They followed the course of the Elk River until the land became more open and the buffalo more abundant. The young men kept food in each camp, racing after the white-rumped antelope and firing arrows into their hearts when they could. The skins were carefully preserved to be tanned and made into clothes.

When the group arrived at the area selected for the camp, the people found their spots and prepared to set up their tepees. Military society members policed the procedure, seeing that everyone was in his place. The women unloaded the travois and sent the horses to graze on the high buffalo grass. Then they raised thirty-foot poles and stretched the richly decorated buffalo hides around them. Because it was hotter here than in the mountains, the flaps were left open to provide circulation.

Tall Bull and Raven hung many scalp locks from the top pole on the outside of their tepee, signifying that a great warrior lived here. Raven and Sweet Grass spread robes and furs around the interior and set up the family's implements of living so that everything would be ready for habitation.

The Wolves went out to spot the herds and check for enemies. The military society members, taking turns, posted guards around the camp to prevent surprise attacks. The people were not as well protected on the plains as they were in their mountain valley.

The first night, Tall Bull met with the members of his society, the Foxes. They all sat around the fire in Elk Heart's tepee and smoked, talking about buffalo hunts of the past. When Tall Bull returned home, he sat in front of the glowing embers of the fire and went into a trance. Cougar Woman sat quietly in the background with Raven and Sweet Grass. Soon Tall Bull began to murmur to himself and then he broke into song, rocking back and forth. He took a small drum and began to beat it, chanting to his hawk medicine to help him in the hunt. He asked for many buffalo for the people this winter.

Tall Bull liked to hunt buffalo. He and other hunters would kill them, and then the women would come to take care of the carcasses. The military societies would see that the meat was distributed evenly so no one would go hungry. If one of the hunters got too rambunctious or scared the herd, the society members would beat him severely for his action. Everything was controlled for the good of all.

While Cougar Woman watched the swaying figure of Tall Bull, she fingered the fine cedar bow he had given her when she outgrew her little one. It could send an arrow through a deer, and she hoped it could send one straight to the heart of a buffalo. She knew Tall Bull would let her try, although it was very dangerous. She was old enough now. Perhaps he would even let her ride by his side as he chased the great beasts on his spotted horse. Bold Eagle had permission from Elk Heart to ride after the buffalo, but she hadn't asked yet.

Tall Bull set his drum aside and took his bone bow. It was a powerful weapon, about three feet in length and capable of sending an arrow with incredible force. His was a special bow. Most warriors had bows of cedar like the one he had given to Cougar Woman. These were short and could be easily handled from the back or side of a horse.

Tall Bull took out his arrows and looked them over for flaws. He had two types: one for men and another for game. The former had slightly weakened barbs that stayed inside the victim to fester and cause death; the latter could be pulled out easily and used over and over again. Tall Bull felt the bone points to test their sharpness and then put them back into the elkskin quiver that Raven had spent many days decorating with porcupine quills and fringe.

In the morning Tall Bull would have her wrap his long hair in otter skin strips and tie it up so it wouldn't get in his way during the serious business of the hunt. Then he would strip down and take his bow with eight or ten arrows and braided rawhide rope. A buffalo hunter wanted few encumbrances.

Cougar Woman readied her bow and hunting arrows, and plaited a rope especially for the hunt. It would hang from her horse and drag at least twelve feet behind so that if she were thrown, she could grab it to catch her horse. Anyone on foot in the herd was in grave danger if the animals began to run. Buffalo didn't like the smell of humans, and seemed to sense trouble when they were on foot. They were not so skittish around humans who were mounted. Perhaps, she thought, it was because of all the wild horses that roamed with them on the plains.

Cougar Woman saw Tall Bull look toward her. She crept over and sat next to him. "Father," she began, "I would like to kill buffalo with the hunters. This year I am old enough."

"You—Do you think you can drive your arrow through to the heart of one? Do you know how to position your horse so you can shoot true?"

"Yes, I have power and my aim is perfect."

"Then you shall ride beside me. But remember, if you get into trouble, I will not have time to help you. You will have to take care of yourself. The Foxes police the hunt tomorrow. Do you have everything in readiness?"

"Yes, my arrows are sharp and my horse is ready." Tall Bull grunted his approval and settled back with his pipe before going to sleep. Dawn would come early.

Cougar Woman went to her robe. She barely heard Sweet Grass snoring in the opposite corner of the big lodge he now called his own.

She smiled, remembering what he had told her that afternoon. "You are going to kill three buffalo," he had said, "but do not ride after more. The spirits told me it should be so." Thinking of how Sweet Grass always talked to spirits, she fell asleep.

On the day of the first hunt, the air was charged with excitement. The entire camp was awake before dawn, and the thunder of horses racing through as riders went out made the earth quiver. Tall Bull and Cougar Woman were mounted and on a small hill overlooking the herds before sunup. She pranced her horse around, the animal catching the fever in the air. Tall Bull sat motionless, hoping few warriors would be killed.

A chilly breeze blew the scent of buffalo dung their way. At times the stench was overpowering, as if the damp earth held generations of buffalo droppings. Thousands of beasts were milling around. Some were rolling in wallows, and others grunting and pawing the earth to stir up dust or find an appetizing piece of greenery. The herd never seemed to sleep, but they were calm and that was good, because when the herd ran it was as if the whole earth quaked with fear.

The Foxes met and deployed their members to the side of a small group of buffalo. These had been marked for the day's hunt. All the hunters were ready and moved quietly into position. Daylight was beginning to break in the east with strips of pink and gold as the sun came over the edge of their world.

Cougar Woman stayed near Tall Bull. Elk Heart was close by, as was Bold Eagle who, seeing Cougar Woman, waved his bow in greeting. She noticed that he was on Elk Heart's best horse while Elk Heart was on a stolen Dakotah horse. Tall Bull rode his spotted horse, and she, like Elk Heart, had chosen a black Dakotah—the one with lightning on his face.

The hunters let their rawhide ropes trail and moved into the herds. The shaggy beasts did not yet sense anything wrong. Then someone sent the first arrow and the scream of the wounded buffalo alerted the rest of the herd. They were off.

Cougar Woman wheeled her horse and charged after Tall Bull. Bold Eagle was behind her to the right where she could see him. In her left hand she held three arrows and her bow, ready to draw. Her rawhide quirt hung from her wrist. The black horse's rein dangled on his neck and she guided him with her legs. The horse knew what to do and raced up alongside a large bull. As the horse came up on the right side of the buffalo, Cougar Woman slipped an arrow on her bow and drew it back. The pounding of the running beast and its strong smell reached her highly charged senses. Her excitement was almost overwhelming. She yelled at the top of her lungs, encouraging her mount. Her horse began to outrun the buffalo, and just as it came ahead of the bull she shot her arrow into the beast. She veered her horse sharply aside in case the beast, with its lowered horns, tried to gouge her mount. She whipped her horse with the bow to make him move faster, and turned to see the buffalo stumble and fall. She felt a great sense of elation. With one arrow she had killed her first buffalo.

Keeping her horse at a full gallop, she was able to approach Bold Eagle who was chasing a buffalo. His horse was just keeping up with the racing bull. She dropped behind to see him kill it. Then to her horror, his horse stepped in a hole and pitched forward, sending Bold Eagle flying to the ground. The buffalo were running and she knew Bold Eagle would be trampled to death if something was not done fast. She raced toward him, trying to get there before a small herd would arrive and run over his body. He saw her coming. Knowing what terrible danger he was in, Bold Eagle began running to meet her. She slowed her horse as she approached him, and he vaulted up behind her. As he leaned on her back she heard him sigh and felt his grateful hug. He's only had the wind knocked out of him, she thought, and kept her horse moving until they got to the outside of the herds.

There was no need to try to get Bold Eagle's horse. It had broken a leg and was being dispatched by a passing warrior. And the buffalo, in their frenzy to escape, were running over its body. Elk Heart would be saddened to lose it.

"We'll have to steal more horses," Cougar Woman said, trying to make light of the tense situation.

Bold Eagle was downcast. "You saved me again. I will do the same for you if the spirits will let me."

Ignoring his comment, she offered, "Tomorrow you can ride one of my black Dakotah horses. They are both trained to hunt buffalo."

He nodded in gratitude and they returned to camp riding double.

That night there was much feasting and dancing. The rich aroma of roasting buffalo meat filled the air, and the beat of the drums echoed across the open plains. The entire village was celebrating the first day of the hunt. They were also asking for protection for the following days. Only one man had been seriously hurt; his horse had thrown him and an enraged buffalo had gored him in the stomach, ripping it open. Despite the medicine man's incantations, it was doubtful that the rider would survive.

Cougar Woman and Bold Eagle joined Tall Bull to watch the dancing figures in the flickering lights of a huge campfire. The drums were thunderous, she thought, probably letting all their enemies know where they were. It was a large camp, however, and not too many would attack.

The Lumpwoods were protecting the camp that night. They, like the Foxes and the War Clubs, were a military society. In another year, both she and Bold Eagle would join a military society and go on organized war parties. They would probably become Foxes, because Tall Bull and Elk Heart were members. Tall Bull was an honored man indeed, a great and wise warrior. He had also killed several buffalo that day, and had been pleased to see Cougar Woman kill a big bull.

"Do not turn your horse too sharply," he told her. "It could stumble, causing you great trouble." She knew that from Bold Eagle's experience.

The next day when she went on another hunt, she remembered what Tall Bull had told her and was careful not to swerve her horse too sharply to escape the charging buffalo. That morning she had taken some of her cougar medicine and smeared it on her face for protection. Then she had gone to catch the second black Dakotah horse for Bold Eagle. She intended to ride the lightning one again. It had done well yesterday. Tall Bull had left by the time she and Bold Eagle started out together.

They rode to the top of a small hill where they could see other riders starting after the selected herd. The buffalo seemed uneasy. They sensed the Indians after them again and were moving about restlessly. She felt her medicine strongly today. It seemed to form a protective shield around her. When she went on the war trail it would do the same.

The two of them headed toward the herd, watching for any directions the Foxes would give them. Then they saw

Running Fox charge toward a lone bull. He raced after it, but the bull turned on him and thundered at his horse. Running Fox turned his horse roughly and got away. The bull went straight past him.

Cougar Woman smiled to herself. She would not have been unhappy if Running Fox had been run down, she thought. Maybe next time he will not be so lucky!

She picked out her bull and started after it. Her black horse was running easily. The bull began increasing its speed as soon as it felt the horse chasing it. Her horse gradually caught up with the buffalo. As it pulled ahead, she fitted an arrow to her bow and held it ready to shoot, waiting for the right moment. At the last second, the bull changed its pace and her arrow went into its neck, far from the heart. The bull charged at her in fury. She turned her horse and, with the bull after her, galloped away. Fitting another arrow, she veered the horse to the right and whirled to come in behind the bull. As the beast turned on its tormentor again, she was ready and shot another arrow directly into its heart. The bull slumped over and the light faded in its eyes, but Cougar Woman had gone after another bull by then and did not pay any attention.

Sweet Grass had told her to kill only three and that was what she would do. She picked out a smaller one, a cow, and rode it down to have her arrow go right to its mark. Then she rode out of the herds and stopped on a hill to watch.

Bold Eagle was still chasing buffalo and had killed at least one. There were more to be killed before the village would have enough meat for the winter. The women came out with horses on which they would pack the butchered meat and bones. They would leave the hearts as an offering to The One Above so he would make the buffalo plentiful again next year. At times they ate part of the meat raw, but most was cooked or dried.

That day, she knew, the men would dig pits and line them with white-hot rocks. Then they'd cut chokecherry boughs from the stream edges and stack them in the pits with thick chunks of fresh buffalo meat. These would be placed in layers—boughs then meat then boughs, and so on—and sprinkled with water. Each pit would be covered with a buffalo stomach and then with earth. Large fires would burn on top of the pits throughout the night. In the morning when the pits were opened and the smell of the cooked buffalo meat penetrated everything, they would feast again. Thinking about it made her mouth water.

After the women butchered the meat, they cut into strips the parts to be dried and hung the strips in the sun on racks. Surely, she thought, the noisy black and white magpies would come to steal them, but the dogs would protect them, yapping and snarling at the thieving birds. The dry meat would be pounded into pemmican—meat mixed with suet, marrow, and red berries. This stored easily and was nutritious. The marrow and fat would be stored in skins, and the sinews taken for bowstrings and thread. Eventually spoons and cups would be made from the bones. The hides would be cured and used for tepee coverings or clothing, such as warm robes perfect for the freezing winter ahead. Other tribesmen made snowshoes out of buffalo hide strips. The people left very little of the buffalo carcass. Every part served a purpose.

The women worked quickly. They dared not wait too long or the ever-present scavengers, the buffalo wolves and coyotes, would devour the carcasses. These animals followed the herds, as did the evil-bringing vultures. She shuddered at the memory of Bold Eagle lying on the mountain with the vultures circling overhead. They picked bones clean.

The day was exciting. Cougar Woman was proud that she had been able to shoot her arrows straight to make clean kills. When she finally went on the war trail she would do the same.

She saw Sweet Grass and Raven coming over the hill and moving toward a buffalo carcass. She rode out to join them, waving her bow in the air to attract their attention and yelling like a victorious warrior. Her long black hair broke loose from its ties and streamed out behind her. Cougar Woman looked more like the wild child she was than the warrior woman she would soon become.

Part II

4

War Party

SEVERAL WINTERS PASSED AND SPRING WAS UPON THEM. WILLOWS and bushes near the streams were beginning to form leaf buds and the snow was receding on the peaks.

Tall Bull, Raven, Cougar Woman, and Sweet Grass had spent the winter camped in the thick woods of a sheltered valley. About fifty tepees were scattered through the area. Most of the men were members of Tall Bull's military society, the Foxes.

They were all restless after the inactivity forced on them by unusually deep snows. For weeks at a time only the tops of the tepees showed above the drifts.

Elk Heart was the first to emerge. One morning, he and another warrior followed the still-frozen creek looking for game. They got no farther than a few miles when they ran into a group of Poor Lodges, or Flatheads, who had been trapped by blizzards on the Absaroke side of the high mountains. Elk Heart was killed, but his companion managed to escape. The six Poor Lodge warriors were not interested in pursuing one man. They wanted to get home. When the survivor returned to camp, he found Tall Bull and told him of his brother's death.

"We will avenge the death of Elk Heart," Tall Bull said, with a sad heart. "But we will wait until the snows melt. We will bide our time and take our revenge to the heart of the Poor Lodge Nation."

Cougar Woman sat beside him in front of the fire. She pulled her buffalo robe tighter to prevent a cold draught from running down her neck, although it was excitement that made her shiver. She hoped Tall Bull would take her this time. He would lead this war party. It was right that he avenge his brother. Bold Eagle would also go, along with any Foxes who wanted to join.

"First, I will bring my brother's body back. I do not like the idea of the wolves tearing it apart." Tall Bull left the tepee.

It was easy to follow the trail since it had not snowed again. They rode along the creek until they found Elk Heart's body where the Poor Lodges had killed and scalped him. The arrow through his neck was still there. Tall Bull snapped the shaft off and wrapped the corpse in a robe. Then he tied his brother's body on a horse and leaped back up on his own.

When they got back to camp, Tall Bull gave Elk Heart's body to his women. They would prepare it for burial and he would help if they needed him. The women's screams of mourning followed Tall Bull and Cougar Woman back to their own lodge, where Tall Bull cut his hair in grief for his brother. Then he sat alone staring into the fire, thinking how he would lead the war party over the mountains.

Cougar Woman was glad Bold Eagle had not seen his father's body lying out in the snow with its long hair expertly ripped off to decorate the tepee of some Poor Lodge warrior. Bold Eagle would want to chase the Poor Lodges now. Tall Bull's plan was much wiser.

Spring came gradually. There were a few final snowstorms, but they did not last. Meanwhile, preparations were going on for the weeks-long excursion across the mountains into the country of the Poor Lodges. They would avenge Elk Heart and bring back horses.

Cougar Woman was pleased. Tall Bull had accepted her offer to come along as a helper. He also allowed her to assist him in making arrows and preparing equipment. They chose straight cherry branches from bundles hanging in the tepee to season. She sanded them smooth by pulling them through two grooved pieces of sandstone shaped for an arrow shaft. Afterward, they stuck buzzard feathers on the shafts and notched the ends. Lastly, they fitted their sharp arrow points and strapped them firmly in place with rawhide twine.

For a year Tall Bull had left the business of war to the young men and had spent his time making medicine. Now he was impelled to go, but unlike the brash young men who would rush after six enemies, he would wait and make his stroke count where it hurt most. Cougar Woman was learning from him.

The horses were beginning to lose their shaggy winter coats when Tall Bull called together all the warriors who would go to the country of the Poor Lodges. First, their band would join another Absaroke camp near the Elk River. After that, the war party would go through friendly Atsina country. From there they would move along the east side of the mountains to a pass over the spine of the highest peaks and go into Poor Lodge country. On their return, they would follow the melting snows so they could bring horses back easily.

The criers ran through the village one bright June morning. "Pack up! We move to the camp of our relatives the Many Lodges near the Elk River. Pack up! We move today!"

Tall Bull rode in front with the honored men and chiefs while Raven and Sweet Grass rode on two of the horses pulling the many travois that carried their belongings. Cougar Woman, Bold Eagle, and a younger brother of his called Crooked Nose drove their family herds.

The going was tough. In many places ice and snow lingered on the north sides of the slopes. There was mud, too,
bogging down the horses and splashing up on the laden
travois. When they came to the swollen waters of a river, they
noticed debris was being swept along by the swift current.
The line stopped while the chiefs pondered the situation.

They decided to cross. There was no other way at this
time of year. Tall Bull gave the signal by raising his long pipe
and pointing across the torrent.

Everyone set about collecting driftwood and fashioning it
into rafts to which the ends of the lodge poles were attached
and all the belongings strapped on. The old women and children were put on top, where they held tightly to the rawhide
thongs lashing the pile to the poles. Then the young men
pushed the rafts into the rushing current.

The young women swam behind, holding the ends of the
long lodge poles on the downstream side of each raft. Horses
swam with young men holding on to their manes and guid-
ing them. Bold Eagle crossed beside his family, and Cougar
Woman swam her spotted pony next to Raven and Sweet
Grass. The current was strong, and a straight course across
was impossible. The water was like ice and full of logs and
other trash swept along as the river rose from the snowmelt.

Before getting in the water, they had stopped to paint red
stripes around their wrists, ankles, and waists as protection
against the fierce water monsters who lived in this raging
stream. Sweet Grass had also made Raven take off her white
beads for fear of aggravating the monsters. The beads, repre-
senting hailstones, were a symbol of the thunderbird, a deadly enemy of the aquatic spirits. This simple procedure went a
long way toward guaranteeing their safe passage.

On the travois next to them a family was grieving loudly.
Their aged grandmother had refused to cross. She had
screamed her fears, and despite efforts by her daughter and
grandchildren to reassure her, had grabbed a knife and plunged

it into her heart. Her time came quickly, after which they put her body in a small cave, walling it up with boulders to keep scavengers away. This slowed the tribe's progress, but soon the process of crossing was under way again.

Several horses were swept away in the current. The riders, hit by floating debris, let go and the horses on their own went with the stream flow. Aside from minor mishaps, Raven's lodge and their herd got across, as did most others.

The Many Lodges were camped in the river valley. When Tall Bull's band arrived, they put their tepees at the end of the lines that paralleled a creek coming off the river.

Tall Bull told the principal chief, Weasel Bear, who wintered with this group of Many Lodges, of his plan to go to the land of the Poor Lodges. Everyone wished the war party good luck, and there was much dancing and celebrating. They were delighted to be together after the long winter and were happy for the warriors who would have a chance to avenge Elk Heart.

In Tall Bull's tepee, Fox Society members met several nights in a row. They sang special medicine songs and received instructions from Tall Bull. Swift Bear, Two Fingers, and One Ear were appointed by Tall Bull to be Wolves, or scouts. All were seasoned warriors and had been over the mountains before. They knew the route as well as something about their enemies who, with the Striped Feathered Arrows, counted among the bravest. Bold Eagle and Cougar Woman were selected as helpers. They would learn by assisting the warriors. This was not easy, but it served as an apprenticeship in the business of war. As pipeholder and leader, Tall Bull made all the major decisions. The Wolves were to go out and scout ahead and to the sides of the large party. Their responsibility was to keep Tall Bull informed of everything—especially any movements of the enemy.

The warriors had been instructed to stay away from women and to avoid weakening or disturbing their medicine.

Even Tall Bull abstained from his usual loving sessions with Raven for a week before he left. Cougar Woman knew this, for she was always aware of their actions. Sometimes on nights when she couldn't sleep, either because of Tall Bull's snores or because of his lovemaking with Raven, she'd take her robe and go outside to lie under the stars and dream. On nights like those, she'd remember the starlike lights in the cougar's cave and think she must go again to seek her medicine.

The night before they were to go, Tall Bull lingered in front of the dying fire after the Foxes had left. He motioned to Cougar Woman to sit beside him. His eyes were kind as he addressed her.

"Tomorrow you shall go on your first war party. Keep your eyes and ears open. There is much you will learn. You shall go on many more and you will do well. I have seen that you shall take your first scalp on this journey. Now go to bed. We leave at sunset on our strongest horses."

He blew the smoke from his pipe toward Father Sky and toward Mother Earth before putting it down and pulling his robe close about him. Cougar Woman noticed as she rolled up in her fur robe that Tall Bull's head had dropped forward on his chest. The flickering light from the embers shone on his graying hair that Raven had already lovingly bound in thin otter skins to keep it manageable. Cougar Woman went to sleep with the smell of wood smoke in her nostrils as a brisk breeze whipped some smoke back inside the tepee.

The next morning Sweet Grass gave Cougar Woman two pairs of new moccasins. As he handed them to her, he said softly, "You will wear these in safety. Your cougar medicine is powerful. The spirits told me you will soon become a warrior." Before she could answer, he slipped silently back into the lodge.

The war party headed west toward the Elk River. There were twenty-five of them—not the largest war party by any means, but all eager to steal Poor Lodge horses and to avenge Elk Heart.

The three Wolves scouted ahead although they were still in Absaroke territory and chances they'd meet an enemy force were very small. Once they started up the great northern trail on the east side of the high mountains to the three forks of the Big River, they had to watch out for Pecunies, their deadly enemies. Even in the country of their Atsina allies, the Wolves had to stay alert.

Cougar Woman and Bold Eagle rode behind Tall Bull, ready to do his bidding. As helpers, they did anything the warriors asked. They were also subject to a certain amount of hazing. However, everything that happened on the war party was secret—only members knew about it. Everything, that is, except for counting coup and reciting brave deeds that were told to others for purposes of establishing prestige.

They rode most of the first night and all the next day, finally camping on the Elk River where it came out of the mountains. The following day they crossed the Elk and headed north toward the Big River and eventually the pass that took them into the country of the Poor Lodges.

By now the Wolves were going out all day. Upon sighting an enemy they were to let out a wolf howl to alert the main party. They were so well-camouflaged that Cougar Woman and Bold Eagle had trouble recognizing them. The first one who came in to report to Tall Bull was One Ear. His body was smeared with mud that had dried to the gray color of a wolf. On his head he had fashioned two pointed ears. He wore a full wolf skin with its head on the back of his own. When One Ear crept on the ground, he looked so much like a wolf that no one bothered him. Cougar Woman was fascinated. Bold Eagle wanted to be a Wolf instead of a helper. Tall Bull was pleased that the way was clear and sent One Ear out again.

Cougar Woman rode behind Tall Bull. She was elated. She looked at her shield made from the thick hide of an old buffalo bull and strong enough to turn the sharpest arrow. On its deerskin covering she had painted the picture of a cougar, her medicine. She knew it made her a strong warrior with nothing to fear. She wore a war shirt made from her cougar skin. Her medicine bag was hanging from her belt, along with a sharp knife.

Cougar Woman fingered her medicine bundle. She had taken great pains to dry the cougar heart well and mix the powdered substance with sweet grass and red dye made from berries. This she used as special medicine before leaving, eating a small bit and smearing some on her face in lightninglike lines.

Again she felt around her a field of protection no arrow could penetrate. She hoped Tall Bull would allow her to count coup against the enemy. She wanted to be able to wear a scalp shirt and foxtails on her moccasin heels.

Bold Eagle was riding beside her. He was quiet and she wondered if he was as pleased as she. "Bold Eagle," she called to him. "Are you wishing you were the appointed Wolf, instead of One Ear?"

"Yes." He looked at her and moved his horse closer. They were riding through a broad valley. Jagged peaks covered the western horizon as far as they could see. There was a lot of game—buffalo, elk, antelope, and deer—but the valley floor was dry, not as lush as their own favored mountain area. Jackrabbits sprang up in front of them and raced away leaving little puffs of dust. "I wonder when we'll see our first Poor Lodge warrior. They are said to be tall and courageous."

"I'll be happy to see one so I can start collecting scalps."

He agreed by nodding his head. "What did Sweet Grass say?"

"Sweet Grass told me we would be successful although we'd lose several warriors. He said we'd get some fine horses. I'd *like* some more." She looked at the Dakotah lightning. She could stand a faster horse.

"Yes, I need some, too, but we're only helpers and may not get a chance to steal any."

"We will if we take it." She was thinking about a dark horse Sweet Grass had told her about. "Very fleet of foot," he had said. "It can outrun anything we have. You will find it tied to a chief's lodge next to a stream. Take it and its speed will help you escape many dangers. There will be eagle feathers in its black mane and tail, but its body will be brown." She knew she would find this horse but she did not know when.

A wolf howl came back to them, and then another. Tall Bull signaled them to stop. Ahead they could see a large trail of dust, and she guessed that someone was chasing a herd of buffalo. They waited until Tall Bull heard from a Wolf she didn't recognize. He galloped up, gave Tall Bull his report, and rode away.

Tall Bull changed their direction, and they rode toward the knife-edged range of mountains. He did not want anything to deter them from their main objective: revenge.

It took several days to reach the high pass that would take them over the spine to where the rivers run in the opposite direction. The snow was just melting off the trail and it was muddy and slippery. She was glad her horse was surefooted. Driving a herd back over this would be difficult, she thought, although the pass was wide.

There were many birds. Geese going north almost blackened the skies as they climbed up into the pass. Eagles were everywhere.

The wind howled around the sharp ledges, and snow-covered heights with steep granite sides towered over them. Through the snow, green shoots of alpine plants were beginning to appear. Waterfalls from melting snows raced down crevasses and crossed the trail, washing out sections of it. Cougar Woman breathed deeply of the rarefied air and pulled her buffalo robe tighter. It was cold.

As they came out of the pass, the trail widened, and below they could see a broad plain stretching to far mountains. Once on the level they turned north and rode fast. There was game of every kind. The land was green and the slopes were covered with huge trees. The jagged gray peaks beyond went into the sky like giant teeth. The Poor Lodges had magnificent country. She wondered why they came into Absaroke lands to hunt.

The Wolves had gone ahead. One returned late in the afternoon to report a large Poor Lodge village by the shores of a great lake. Tall Bull was pleased. This was what he'd been waiting for. In a vision, he'd seen this war party surprise a large Poor Lodge village by a lake, steal a sizable horse herd, and kill many men.

Cougar Woman and Bold Eagle were told to take care of the horses as Tall Bull led one group of warriors to the village. Another group went to steal part of the herd grazing near the east side of the enemy tepees. They were to drive them down the valley and start them through the pass before helping the others hold off any Poor Lodges chasing them.

Night came and, surprisingly, they had not been discovered. Bold Eagle and Cougar Woman were restless and wished they could do something more exciting than hold horses. Soon they heard screams and shouts and then the sound of many hooves as the warriors assigned to capturing the enemy's horses thundered past their hiding place racing toward the pass. Two Fingers appeared and yelled, "Get on your horses and run for the pass. The others are coming and so is a Poor Lodge war party." He urged his horse and one he'd stolen into a gallop, vanishing in the darkness.

Bold Eagle leaped on his mount and looked at Cougar Woman. "As helpers we must do as we are told." He waited for her to get on her horse.

"I know, but I do not want to leave Tall Bull behind. You go."

Alarmed by her response, he said, "You may get caught, or die."

She turned her back on him and started toward the village, leading her horse. The moon was out and she could see figures running toward her. She stepped behind some trees and waited with her knife ready. As they ran past she recognized Tall Bull and followed.

In the distance she heard the shouts of the pursuing Poor Lodges. Tall Bull ordered a few warriors under One Ear to defend the entrance to the pass. The rest he kept moving. They helped drive the stolen horses over the mountains. Some horses straggled behind and were left, but all together they had over a hundred.

Fighting the dirt and grit behind the climbing horses, Cougar Woman wondered about her first scalp and that fast horse. So far, she hadn't seen a Poor Lodge warrior, and certainly not a chief's tepee with a horse beside it.

They kept going until they were on their own side of the mountains. Then Tall Bull sent half his warriors under the direction of Swift Bear home with the horses. Turning to the other half he said, "Now we shall wait for the Poor Lodges and kill them."

Tall Bull had his warriors hide behind rocks and look down on a narrow section of the trail coming through the mountains. "We can rest and eat, but be alert for our brothers first. They will lead the Poor Lodges into our arrows."

Cougar Woman crouched down next to Tall Bull. She was exhausted and marveled at his stamina. Tall Bull was no longer young, although his massive form was still powerful and did not show his years. He set his arrows out and signaled to her to do likewise. "We will be ready for them. Now rest. You will get your first scalp soon."

She closed her eyes and didn't know anything until a wolf howl split the silence, then another. In the early dawn light she could see their few warriors who had been left behind come running through the pass. Hard on their heels came a Poor Lodge war party yelling and whooping but not expecting an ambush. The Poor Lodge warriors *were* tall men. Tall Bull shot his arrow and killed the leader, who fell off his horse, clutching at the feathered shaft in his throat.

Cougar Woman waited until a warrior came closer. Then she sent her arrow into his chest, quickly fitting another arrow to her bow. Everyone was shooting regularly and the Poor Lodges were falling. Then they turned and ran back through the pass. Cougar Woman was more elated than ever.

Tall Bull motioned to her to follow him as he got up and ran to the nearest fallen enemy. He took out his knife, saying, "Watch. Learn how to scalp. When you have collected enough, you will have a shirt like mine, decorated with the hair of your enemies."

He took the dead man's hair in his left hand, lifting the head off the ground. With his right he took his knife and expertly ran it around the scalp line. With one wrench, he ripped the hair from the Poor Lodge's head. "Go. Do your own," he said to her as he moved to another.

Cougar Woman knelt by a dead Poor Lodge. Following Tall Bull's instructions, she took her sharp knife and scalped him. She had trouble ripping the hair off, but solved the problem by putting her moccasined foot on the dead man's neck and pulling hard. She took her fresh scalp and, leaping on her horse, raced out of the pass toward Absaroke country taking the trail made by the horse herd. The other warriors followed. They would catch up with the captured herd and drive them into camp. She looked forward to rest and fresh food. The journey had been successful, although she still had not gotten that fast horse.

The victory celebration was noisy and excited. Everyone in the village turned out to hail the successful war party. Tall Bull led them, wearing his warbonnet and scalp shirt with human hair tufts down the sleeves and across the chest. Waving her fresh scalp, Cougar Woman cavorted her horse behind him. The huge captive herd milled around, creating more confusion.

That night the Absaroke held a scalp dance. The drums

beat through the night while the women danced with the scalps.

Hi-Ya, Hi-Ya, Hi-Ya-Hi-Hi-Hi-Hi

The warriors smoked and told about their bravery. Cougar Woman could hardly wait to be a full warrior.

Sweet Grass had congratulated her on her scalp, which he took to dance with. "You have done as you were supposed to, but you must still find the fast horse. It is waiting for you."

She felt uncomfortable because she had not fulfilled the entire vision, but Sweet Grass thought it all right and consoled her.

Swift Bear passed her in the dark behind a tepee. He joked and slapped her on the shoulder. "I am after a pretty woman," he said, making an obscene gesture. "Don't tell anyone you saw me."

A little later she saw him taking the wife of Ten Wolves, whose tepee was pitched near theirs. They were giggling together and Swift Bear, with his arm about her waist, was leading her into the woods. Apparently he had slept with her before she married Ten Wolves. In fact, most of the victorious Foxes were kidnapping women they had slept with before marriage, as was their custom. The whole camp was raucous with merriment. She wondered if Bold Eagle had found a girl he wanted.

Cougar Woman had no interest in this part of the celebration. She had left the dancing to go to her tepee. A shadow confronted her in the dark. It was Running Fox.

"At last, the warrior woman without her loyal Bold Eagle." She could see his smirking face in her mind. His voice was insulting. She sensed he meant trouble. Running Fox moved closer to her until she could feel the heat of his breath on her forehead. "We'll see how much woman you are." He reached out for her but she jumped back and whipped out her knife.

"If you come any closer, I'll kill you." Her voice was low and menacing. She felt her face heat up with fury.

He hesitated, wondering if she really meant it.

She followed her advantage. "Running Fox, I can kill you easily. Do not tempt me, because it would please me to hang your scalp on my lodge pole to remind me of one so foul that even birds of death would not pick his bones."

He let out a nasty laugh. "Can't you take a joke? Who would want a woman as cold as you!" He turned and faded into the darkness.

She breathed more easily. Someday she would kill him, but now she wanted to be alone with her thoughts. Taking her horse, she rode out of camp to a hill where she could look down on the village. The sounds of dancing and the flickering firelight would let anyone know the Absaroke were celebrating. May they always be so happy, she thought, sitting in the grass.

Looking at the many stars in the dark robe of the sky, she thought about her future leading war parties to fame, the way her vision had predicted. She heard a night bird and then another. A coyote howled off to her left. Everything seemed peaceful. As she watched, a star fell, then several more. Soon a shower of stars with their bright twinkling lights dropped through the black sky. Cougar Woman was frightened. She moved back against her waiting horse. Was The One Above telling her something? The noise in the village ceased.

When the display in the sky was over, she rode back to the village. People were in their tepees, frightened of something they did not understand. As she rode to her lodge she sensed people peeking out at her. Tall Bull and Raven were inside.

Tall Bull greeted her. "The stars fell upon you when you were outside. You should have extraordinary powers now."

She did not feel any different, but if he believed it, perhaps he was right. Cougar Woman, remaining silent, wrapped herself in her buffalo robe and went to sleep.

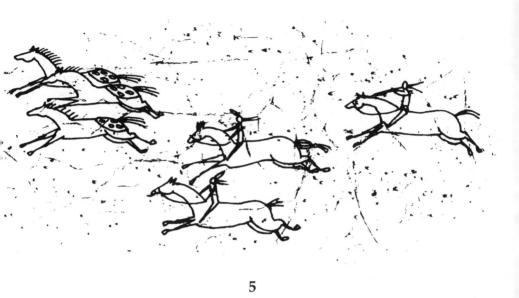

5

The Spotted Horses

COUGAR WOMAN WANTED MORE HORSES OF HER OWN. SHE wanted good horses and knew that the Nez Percé over the mountains had the finest. She had always liked Tall Bull's spirited horse but, like Tall Bull, it was getting old. She decided to see if Bold Eagle would go with her, and she found him by his tepee working on new arrows.

"It is a good day to plan a raid on the Nez Percé for some fine horses," she told him in greeting.

Bold Eagle put aside the arrow he was working on. He looked at her. She had on a new pair of antelope skin leggings with side fringes and a new shirt. He admired Sweet Grass's fine quillwork decorating the front of the shirt with a blood red circle like a rising sun. He really needed a wife to make his clothes and keep his lodge, he thought. Perhaps if he did well on a trip across the mountains, he could get enough horses to buy a pretty woman, although he had no particular one in mind. Looking at Cougar Woman, he said, "I need more horses. When shall we go?"

"Tomorrow. We can get our weapons and medicine ready today." She was pleased Bold Eagle would go. They worked well together. "I will tell Sweet Grass to put out my extra moccasins." She returned to Tall Bull's lodge.

Sweet Grass was on his knees helping Raven pound chokecherries into mash. This would be dried and stored in parfleches for winter use. He stopped when Cougar Woman appeared and looked up at her. "You will be leaving camp for several weeks," he said uncannily. "I shall prepare your moccasins and parfleches. Bring back many horses."

Cougar Woman was used to Sweet Grass's psychic abilities. "I leave in the morning," she told him. She went to find Tall Bull, whom she had seen sitting on a hillside overlooking the village. He was leaning against a boulder smoking his pipe. When he saw her coming, he took the pipe out of his mouth and offered it to her.

She sat beside him and drew on the pipe, admiring the red stone bowl he had carved in the shape of a buffalo bull. She blew the smoke slowly toward the sky. "This is for my Father, the Sky," she said gravely. "May he guide me on the journey across the mountains to the land of the Nez Percé." Then she took another puff and blew the smoke toward the ground. "This is for my Mother, the Earth. May she protect her child from harm." She passed the pipe to Tall Bull.

He smoked for a few moments without saying anything. As his eyes glazed over slightly, he took a long draw, blowing the smoke slowly in front of him as he exhaled. "You will have a good journey and will bring back many horses. Beware of any white men you meet. Do not trust them." He smoked a few minutes longer.

"I shall give you some of my hawk medicine," he added. "It will protect you along with your own. Do you know where to find the Nez Percé?" He wanted to help her as much as he could.

"We go across the mountains as we did with you, father.

Then we follow the great river farther toward the setting sun, away from the land of the Poor Lodges and north of our enemies the Snakes. We shall have no trouble finding the owners of the spotted war horses."

"No, but ride your fleetest horse and do not take bold chances. The Nez Percé are fine horsemen and will chase you. They prize their horses more than their women."

She listened carefully to him, thinking they would look things over by day and steal horses in the dark of night. There would be some light, as the moon was beginning to wane. "Tell me, father, do you see the camp of the Nez Percé?"

Tall Bull drew on his pipe, blowing the smoke near the ground. He stared into it as the breeze wafted it away. "Their village is by a wide river. There is a large meadowland and they have set their lodges up by the water. There are many tepees there. They are in the summer grazing land. I see thousands of spotted ones with many young. Look—see the great dust cloud raised by their hooves?" Tall Bull pointed a bronzed arm toward a puff of smoke traveling along the ground. "They guard their horses well. Remember that."

No more was said for some time. Finally, Cougar Woman got up. "I am going to prepare myself," she said.

Tall Bull nodded and continued to smoke, watching her as she trotted down the hill toward their tepee. He wished he were younger and could go with her.

Inside the darkened tepee, she went to her bed. She took her medicine bundle from the pole where it hung and, kneeling on the buffalo robe, opened it up. She laid out her small package of cougar heart, a grizzly bear ear, a tiny wizened kingfisher bound in rawhide, and several more special and sacred items that made up her medicine. She checked her red dye. Sitting immobile for many minutes, she prayed to her cougar helper for cunning and courage to go to the country of their enemies. Then she carefully wrapped her medicine bundle up and put it with her weapons and buffalo robe. Sweet

Grass would see that she had several pairs of extra moccasins and sufficient clothing. She picked up a small light saddle stuffed with dried grass and buffalo hair and, taking the decorated blanket she used under it, went out to catch her fastest horse, the Dakotah lightning.

Cougar Woman and Bold Eagle traveled light. They wore skin leggings and shirts and displayed their medicine. Bold Eagle had his eagle feathers tied to his hair so they fell behind his ear in a fantail. Cougar Woman wore her cougar skin shirt, as well as a single eagle feather in her hair to signify a previous coup. Both carried their medicine bundles on their belts. On their bow arms, each had a shield. Neither carried a lance, as it was more in the way than not on an exploit that called for stealth. They had both tied their hair in skins to contain it. Cougar Woman had hers wrapped in rawhide strips down her back. Bold Eagle's was done in similar fashion.

They rode all day and night until they came to the base of the pass. So far they had seen no one. They found a secluded canyon with a gentle waterfall where they camped to rest their horses. Bold Eagle shot a deer, and they ate well and cooked some venison to take with them, careful to make a low fire that could not be seen. They took turns sleeping so they couldn't be taken by surprise if an enemy was in the area.

The following day they started up the rocky trail that led over the highest peaks into the western country of the Poor Lodges and the Nez Percé. As before, the wind was sharp and howled round the peaks like a wolf searching for its lost mate. Still they saw no one, so they kept a steady pace. Neither Cougar Woman nor Bold Eagle wanted to talk. They were saving their energies for the Nez Percé.

As they came across the divide through the mountains, they could see the river far below twisting about like a confused snake. Cougar Woman wondered if it was the one they would follow. They walked their horses much of the time now, resting them.

One evening as they sat against a rock eating, Cougar Woman heard something unusual. Motioning to Bold Eagle, she grabbed her weapons and ran into the trees. He followed but went off to her left, where he could watch the trail as it came around a bend in the cliff. She sneaked closer to the bend and waited. She could distinguish hoofbeats of a horse as it climbed the rocks. A lone rider was following them. They waited.

Suddenly Bold Eagle shouted, "Don't shoot! It's Crooked Nose." He shook his head angrily. He had told his brother to stay home. The boy was lucky Cougar Woman had not shot him.

Crooked Nose rode up to them. "I have come to join you," he said. "I could not stay home with both of you gone."

Bold Eagle scowled, wondering whether to send him back or let him stay. "You are only a boy and should be home. Neither of us has the time to look after you."

The boy looked downcast. He had known Bold Eagle would be mad but decided to come nonetheless. "I shall do as you tell me," he promised. "I won't be in your way. I can gather firewood and hold your horses—anything." He pleaded with them.

Cougar Woman ignored it all and went back to eating. As long as Bold Eagle took care of Crooked Nose, she didn't care that he was with them. He might even come in handy. Bold Eagle finally gave in.

Several days later the threesome came to the river. As they followed it they were careful to avoid open areas where they could be exposed to enemy eyes. At one point they found an old campsite. After exploring it, Cougar Woman said, "A large village must have been here. There were many horses. They have eaten all the grass in the area. A camp with so many horses must move often."

Bold Eagle looked around. "I hope we can get some of them soon," he said impatiently. They had been gone a long time and had yet to see the Nez Percé and their famous horses.

That afternoon, Cougar Woman saw eagles flying ahead of them. She signaled to Bold Eagle. "Look how those birds are disturbed. Someone must be ahead. I'll ride out and see." She urged her horse on and soon came to a hill. Getting off her horse, she cautiously approached the top where she could see for great distances. On a broad grassy plain below her were thousands of horses—the herd of the Nez Percé. She lay in the grass, secure in the knowledge that no one could see her beneath the grass head-covering she wore. She could smell wood smoke on the air and knew the camp was not far away.

Cougar Woman admired the large herd. There were many mares and foals, just as Tall Bull had said. A lot of them were the unusual spotted horses that the Nez Percé were known for, but there were many others—pintos, blacks, roans, chestnuts, bays, even pure white ones. Loving good horseflesh as she did, Cougar Woman became eager and struggled to control herself. She could hardly wait to get into the herd and steal as many as she could. But that would not be wise. Some of the best horses were probably tethered by the owners' lodges where they were safe from thieves. She crept back to the Dakotah lightning and rode to tell Bold Eagle.

He could hardly wait to see the horses. They rode to the hill and, leaving Crooked Nose with their horses, crawled to the crest and lay watching the peaceful herd.

Bold Eagle touched her arm and pointed. Several horsemen were coming toward the herd from the opposite direction. There didn't seem to be any guards. The people must be sure no one is around to steal them, she thought as she watched the riders. They cut out and roped two large spotted horses, leading them back toward their camp. Then Bold Eagle and Cougar Woman heard drums.

"They must be having a celebration of some sort," she whis-pered to Bold Eagle. "What a fine time to steal their horses."

He nodded in agreement. "It would be good to get race-horses or buffalo horses, not mares with their young."

Cougar Woman agreed. It would be too hard to get away with them. They must go into the village to steal the horses they wanted.

At dusk the threesome rode along the winding river past the Nez Percé herd, taking great care not to spook the horses. Stopping in a willow thicket, they dismounted.

"You stay here, Crooked Nose. If you hear screams and noise, you'll know there is trouble. Leave our horses and ride for your life to the mountains. Do *not* wait for us." Bold Eagle was emphatic, intent on ensuring his brother's safety.

Crooked Nose was beginning to be afraid as the potential danger of being discovered sank in, but he hid his fears. He would be brave like Bold Eagle and Cougar Woman. Suddenly he realized that they had both disappeared without a sound, leaving him standing there alone with the horses and his own fearful thoughts. He sat down to wait and to ask The One Above to protect them all and get them safely home.

Cougar Woman and Bold Eagle crept up on the large Nez Percé camp which, as Tall Bull had seen, was near the river's edge. The Nez Percé were having a celebration in the middle of the village. Judging from the noise, many people were gathered. There was dancing and singing, and most likely horse racing. Perhaps, Cougar Woman thought as she lay watching, that was why the horsemen had roped the two spotted horses earlier in the day.

They stretched out in high grass watching the huge camp and looking for horses worthy of stealing. Cougar Woman touched Bold Eagle's arm and motioned that she was going around the whole area.

She silently moved around the outside of the big village. A sliver of moon was out, but fortunately the light was not

great. Huge fires in the center of the camp sent monster shadows across the tepees. Figures danced wildly to the beating
drums. It took her several hours to look around. There were
at least two hundred lodges and great feasting. The smell of
cooking meat carried to her, and she felt her stomach pinch
with hunger. There was so much revelry going on that
Cougar Woman decided they could walk through the camp
and no one would notice.

At last she crawled back beside Bold Eagle, who rolled
over, knife in hand. "There are many lodges and the people
are getting wilder all the time," she reported. "We must be
careful not to trip over them lying together in the grass."

She chuckled to herself. What a fine time they'd picked.
She got up and moved to the first line of tepees. Most seemed
empty. Bold Eagle was beside her as she ran to the shadow of
the nearest lodge. Listening carefully, all her senses alert, she
heard nothing. They moved farther into the circle to the out-
lines of horses tethered by their owners' lodges—the closer to
the center, the more important the owner and the better the
horse.

She ran her hand up a rope to the first horse's neck and
stroked it softly. Swiftly she cut the rope and moved on to
another, leading the first. She couldn't hear Bold Eagle, but
she knew he was doing the same. When she had three, she led
them quietly away from the tepees. Once out of earshot, she
leaped on the nearest horse and rode to where Crooked Nose
waited. So far she had three good horses—prized ones, she
guessed, judging from where she had taken them.

Bold Eagle returned first and was mounted, waiting for
her. The three wasted no time getting back to the valley where
the herd was. There was no pursuit, but that could change
instantly. She pulled her horse to a stop and asked Bold Eagle,
"Shall we cut a few out of the herd to take as well?"

He thought it risky, but their luck thus far was good. It
must be their combined medicines. He agreed and they rode

into the herd, cutting out only those without young. Then driving about twenty-five horses in front of them, they started for the mountains. Crooked Nose was already well in front with the six they had stolen from the village. They didn't stop for two nights. When daylight came the second day, they were racing for the pass. They knew they were being pursued since they had seen dust from a large band of horsemen, but they were holding their lead. All three changed horses regularly to give their mounts a rest. Neither Cougar Woman nor Bold Eagle had the time to admire the horses they had stolen, but they knew they had done well. They also knew they were outnumbered and could not fight. Their hope was in getting away.

As she rode, Cougar Woman sang in a loud voice to her spotted horse:

My horse be swift in flight,
Even like a bird
Carry me in safety
Away from arrows and my enemy
And you shall be rewarded.

The horse seemed to fly along as they drove the stolen herd into the mountains. Looking back, they could see the Nez Percé gaining on them now that they were climbing.

Cougar Woman called to Crooked Nose: "Take the six horses you have and several more that we will point out to you, and drive them home. Bold Eagle and I will take care of the Nez Percé warriors." She showed him the horses, and he herded them before him until he got in front of the main herd. Then Crooked Nose headed for Absaroke country. He knew he must not stop until he got these fine animals to their village, or until his brother and Cougar Woman caught up with him.

At the top of the pass, Cougar Woman rode beside Bold

Eagle and let the horses slow down. "Let's drive most of these back down at the Nez Percé. When they get to the narrow part of the trail they will have nowhere to go. Then we can escape with the best."

Bold Eagle thought it a fine idea, so they cut out the few they wanted and mounted the best they had. Yelling and howling, they turned the bulk of the herd back toward the west and drove them down the pass toward the oncoming Nez Percé warriors. As the horses gathered speed going downhill, Cougar Woman and Bold Eagle turned and raced toward home, not waiting to find out what happened.

They caught up with Crooked Nose near the Medicine River and put their herd together. They had sixteen horses, all fine animals. Cougar Woman shot an elk and they feasted. It was good to relax and laugh about what might have happened when the Nez Percé warriors met the running herd. They let their horses graze and drink while they took turns guarding them and resting.

Cougar Woman was washing in the river late that afternoon when she heard a leaf crackle. She grabbed her knife. Turning, she came face-to-face with a white trapper dressed in filthy buckskins. He rushed at her with a grin on his bearded face, grabbed her knife arm in his huge hand and, with a wrench that made her grimace in pain, took the knife away. He shoved her back roughly to the ground and said something she didn't understand. Then he dropped his pants and threw himself on her, trying to force her legs apart. His smell was strong and rank like bad meat and sweat.

She struggled with the trapper briefly before sensing an opportunity. Relaxing to make him think he'd get his way, she felt him loosening his grip—just enough for her to drive her knee up between his legs with all the force she could muster. The man let out a scream and doubled up in pain.

Cougar Woman rolled away, grabbed her knife, and plunged it into his back. As soon as she felt his dead weight, she pulled out the knife, kicked his body over, and sliced off his testicles. These she would dry and use to decorate her war shirt. Then she neatly scalped him and left his body there for the birds of death to pick at. Diving into the river, she scrubbed away all traces of the stinking white man. She returned to camp bearing his gun and other tokens of her victory. She set the gun beside the napping Bold Eagle.

It was dusk the following day when they came into their mountain valley. They put on new moccasins and clothing they had brought, and painted their faces. Then waving the white man's scalp with the testicles tied to it, Cougar Woman raced into the village beside Bold Eagle and Crooked Nose, driving the captured herd.

The next day Bold Eagle, pleased with his share of horses and new gun, picked out a handsome white-faced stallion. He would give this horse to One Moon's son for his sister, Swift Water Woman. Bold Eagle did not love this girl, but he needed a woman to take care of his lodge, make his clothes, and do the many things around camp he did not have time for. He was also a strong and virile young man who enjoyed his women when he could get them, so he was not against having one in his lodge at his beck and call.

One evening he took the white-faced horse with a fine new bow and a dozen hunting arrows on its saddle to One Moon's tepee, where he looked for the girl's brother. Bold Eagle gave the horse to him. As he did so, he caught a glimpse of Swift Water Woman peeking around the tepee flap. He ignored her and, after exchanging pleasantries with her brother, Bold Eagle returned home.

The next morning he went out early and shot a fat deer. After bleeding it, he slung it over his shoulder and carried it to One Moon's tepee. He presented the prime buck to Swift Water Woman's mother. Again, he went home.

Later that afternoon One Moon appeared and sat beside Bold Eagle outside his tepee. The old man presented him with a fine pipe. The bowl was made of black stone and carved in the shape of a bear's head. It was decorated with eagle feathers.

Bold Eagle turned the pipe around this way and that, admiring it. It was very beautiful. "This is a fine pipe," he said. "I receive it with gratitude and hope you will accept me as your son-in-law."

One Moon was an ancient warrior. As he sat in the sun beside Bold Eagle, his half-closed eyes seemed to blend in with the millions of lines in his leathery face. "You may have Swift Water Woman as your wife, Bold Eagle. You are a good warrior and may become a chief some day. Come and take her to your tepee." The old man got up with a great deal of effort and shuffled off. Bold Eagle was relieved. It was very easy.

He took several more fine horses to One Moon's tepee that afternoon, but this time he did not leave. When Swift Water Woman came out she was wearing a new ankle-length elk-tooth dress and carrying a bundle with her belongings in it. After nodding to her in greeting, Bold Eagle led her to his tepee where she went inside. He waited and smoked his new pipe for a long time before following her. She was waiting for him, and as it turned out she was experienced in the ways of pleasing a hot-blooded young warrior. When he finally rolled over and went to sleep, he was happy. He now had a woman to see to his many wants.

Cougar Woman presented Tall Bull with two splendid horses. He was very pleased, and they spent many hours riding together through the valley trying out horses from her new herd.

"You did well," he told her after they raced two spotted ones down the grassy trail along the riverbank. "I am proud of your accomplishments."

She acknowledged his praise silently, amused that he did not comment on the white man's testicles she had attached to her scalp shirt like dangles. She knew he noticed them, because he missed nothing. She decided not to pursue the matter.

"Did you know Bold Eagle took a wife?" she asked him. "He needed someone in his lodge."

"Yes, every man needs a woman to do jobs around the lodge and to process the hides. In fact, all warriors need women. You, too, will need women, although Sweet Grass does the work of two. There is no time for a warrior to make clothing or to prepare food. There are too many enemies around. This is the time of the year the Dakotah come to our country and we must be doubly careful. Many years ago the Dakotah sneaked up on our village. This was before we had moved west to the high mountains we now call home. They killed many of our people and took their heads. Then the fearsome Dakotah returned to their homes far to the east, almost to a great water. I was not yet born, but my father told me the story. From then on our people hated and feared 'those that took our heads.' It always pleases me to kill a Dakotah. I shall kill as many as I still can, and have since I was a small boy. Many of the scalps on my war shirt are theirs."

Tall Bull did not have to fan her hatred for the Dakotah. Only too vivid still was her memory of the Dakotah warrior murdering her mother. She yearned for fresh Dakotah scalps, too. When she went east to their lands, it would be revenge and scalps she'd be after, not horses.

6

War Leader and Chief

A TRADING POST HAD BEEN OPERATING AT THE CONFLUENCE OF THE
Elk and Big Horn rivers for many years, but most people of
the Absaroke band did not go there. This pleased Tall Bull. He
did not like white man's goods, and he did not want to trap
and kill the many animals in their country as the white man
encouraged them to do. However, Tall Bull was hard-pressed,
as were other chiefs, to keep his young men in line.

Cougar Woman had seen the post from afar but, although
curious, had not gone down to it. She shared Tall Bull's mis-
givings about the white people and often had battles with
Bold Eagle over it. He did, however, prevail upon her to go
with him to the trading post when he took some prime otter
and beaver pelts he had trapped to trade for a woolen capote
with a hood and a shiny kettle for Swift Water Woman.

Sweet Grass showed interest in the trip when Cougar
Woman told him about Bold Eagle's plan. "I have often
wondered about the trading post. I would like to see the
white man's goods and choose some for myself," Sweet

Grass told her as they ate some buffalo ribs he had grilled over the open fire.

"Do you want to go? There should be no danger. Bold Eagle just wants to trade for a capote and a kettle. We'll return very soon."

"Yes, I shall go with you." He munched on the buffalo ribs, letting the juice drip on his beaded buckskin dress. As Cougar Woman looked at him, she found herself thinking he was just like a woman. His black beard had never come in enough to be plucked out. It was like dark duck down on his cheeks near his ears. He also wore his hair like a woman, shorter than that of most men. He even moved like a woman when he walked.

"Bold Eagle is not telling our honored father, Tall Bull, about the trip. He would be angry and tell Bold Eagle to stick to the ways of our people. We did better before the insidious goods of the white man sapped our strength."

"That is true. However, once the process begins it is difficult to stop. It is like a prairie fire out of control." He considered a moment and continued, "Or like a root fire underground that burns without being seen."

"What will happen, Sweet Grass? Do you see good or bad?"

"I have not seen either lately. My powers fade, or perhaps they are resting and being recharged." He looked at her strangely.

"Tall Bull sees bad times. I do not look forward to it. So many white trappers are in the country now, but Tall Bull doesn't want us to kill them." She smiled to herself, thinking of the one she'd killed. "The Pecunies show no mercy," she added, her eyes narrowing. "They kill as many whites as they can. The Pecunies are right in not letting them overrun their hunting grounds."

Sweet Grass reached for another rib and nodded. He saw more than he let on. "Tall Bull is wise in not fighting the whites. They are too numerous. It is better to be on their side. Most of their enemies are our own."

"I do not agree, but Bold Eagle feels as you do." She shrugged with disgust. They would probably take what they wanted anyhow. One could only hope they'd leave something as it was.

The next morning Bold Eagle, Cougar Woman, and Sweet Grass left with Crooked Nose and two Foxes, hoping to get to the trading post in two days. As they rode, Cougar Woman thought about the whites. It was good to know something about your enemy. This trip to the post would let her see how they conducted their business.

Sweet Grass and Bold Eagle both had piles of furs on their horses. This was for trade. Sweet Grass did not know what he wanted. Maybe several of those shiny kettles—they were good to cook with—or some of the white man's metal needles and colored beads, which were easier to use than porcupine quills. He looked at his elaborately designed quilled moccasins. He had made many pairs for Cougar Woman and had also used red and white quills on her scalp shirt. It was decorated on the shoulders and down the sleeves, and was fringed with human hair she had taken. He was a good craftsman and he enjoyed it. Maybe he'd even get one of those reflecting glasses. He could see himself in it now, almost like looking into a clear mountain stream and seeing his soul look back at him.

Bold Eagle led the group. He had his mind on the white capote he was going to get for winter. It would be easier to use than a buffalo robe, and almost as warm. The hood would cover his head and keep the icy winds from freezing his ears.

When they came to a bluff looking down on the rivers, they could see the wooden stockade surrounding the post. There were tepees all around the outside. Some of the Pecunies and their relatives the Bloods were camped there while they traded.

"There are many Pecunies here," Cougar Woman said

with concern. Even though she was of Pecunie blood, she did not trust the enemies of the Absaroke. Besides, she was riding a racehorse she had stolen from a Pecunie chief. If he was there and recognized his prize mare, there could be trouble.

"Yes," said Bold Eagle, "but no fighting is allowed near the post. The white trader insists upon it." He was calm and assured, for he knew this was so.

"Are you sure?"

He nodded to reassure her and they started down the slopes to the post.

As they rode through the circle of outer tepees surrounding the post, Cougar Woman felt uneasy. Something was wrong. Bold Eagle seemed oblivious, but Sweet Grass hung back, looking with interest at the Pecunies who were jeering at their old Absaroke enemies.

Women and children stood by their lodges staring at the newcomers, and an occasional warrior spat in their direction. Even the Pecunie dogs snarled and snapped at the horses' hooves. They continued toward the post and soon came out into an open space directly in front of the entrance.

Cougar Woman heard a swish by her ear and saw Bold Eagle slump over, a feathered arrow sticking out of his left shoulder. She kicked her horse and raced up to him. Grabbing his horse's reins, she galloped the rest of the distance to the fort. They rode through the entry, which swung shut after them. Once safely inside the compound, she could hear arrows thwacking into its wooden posts.

They got Bold Eagle down from his horse, and Sweet Grass disengaged the arrow. Although it came out with a rending of muscle, Bold Eagle scarcely flinched.

Cougar Woman could hear the howls of the Pecunies outside the stockade calling, "Absaroke dogs, come out and let us kill you. You have stolen too many horses. We want the chief's racer you stole from us. You can hide in there forever, and we'll still be waiting for you."

She looked out and saw five Pecunie warriors racing in a circle, yelling, and shouting. Turning around, she saw the hairy-faced white trader looking at Bold Eagle's wound. He poured some evil-smelling liquid onto it that made Bold Eagle wince with pain.

"They will go away," he said, referring to the circle of warriors. "What do you have to trade?"

Sweet Grass handed him the pelts and went with him to the store.

Cougar Woman knew the Pecunies would wait, and she hoped the two Foxes would join her in fighting them. "Certainly five Pecunies are no match for two Foxes," she taunted them, but they showed no inclination to fight. She was disgusted. "You cowards, I shall show you how an Absaroke warrior acts."

She returned to her horse and, holding her bow tightly, jumped onto its back. To Bold Eagle she said, "I will kill the Pecunie who shot you from behind." Then, asking for the gate to be opened, she gave a blood-curdling yell and raced out of the trading post toward the circling Pecunies.

As she reached the first warrior, she turned her horse sharply and shot an arrow from beneath its neck. Then cutting her racehorse through their circle, she struck the nearest Pecunie across the face with her bow, counting coup as she leaned forward on her mare's neck. The surprised Pecunies, not wanting to kill their chief's prize horse, held their fire. She shot another—now two Pecunies were dead. Changing direction again, she circled the confused warriors and shot a third time. The remaining two riders fled. She recovered two Pecunie bows and raced back to the post. Bold Eagle had struggled to his horse and was at the gate ready to assist her. His brother was trying to restrain him.

"Where did the cowards go?" she asked, sitting on her panting horse.

"To the store. They are looking for whiskey."

"We shall find Sweet Grass and slip away tonight."

"You are right. They will be watching for you. You not only have their chief's best horse but you made fools of them."

"We could have killed them all if those cowards had acted like Absaroke warriors." She sat straight and proud on her horse, her face solemn and cruel with her mouth in a thin line and her eyes cold.

Sweet Grass, hearing the commotion, rushed out with Bold Eagle's capote and several kettles. While loading his horse with the odds and ends he'd picked up, he said to her, "I heard you killed three Pecunies. We must get away. This coup will make you a chief."

Cougar Woman looked at him. "We will wait until dark." She thought he seemed agitated.

The post around them was in a state of general confusion of people and animals. The white trader, whom Cougar Woman recognized as Hairy Face, had skins and buffalo robes piled in heaps by the stockade entrance ready for shipment east. He did a brisk business. There were a few horses tied to the rail in front of his store. His living quarters were behind it. Some Pecunies shuffled around while others sat and smoked, watching the proceedings. A group in the far corner was gambling with plum seed dice. She noticed one Indian, a Blood, lying in a stupor by the steps of the store.

Sweet Grass, calmer now, said, "That is the result of the firewater the white traders sell. It does no good—it only destroys the insides and weakens our people. Under its influence they become useless."

As dusk fell, several fires sprang up inside the stockade, and smells of cooking meat mingled with those of sweat and leather. Drumbeats sounded from the Bloods and Pecunies camped outside.

"I think we should slip away as soon as things quiet down," she said to Bold Eagle, who was eating a piece of meat Sweet Grass had cooked. His brother was squatting beside him. Bold Eagle nodded. They decided to leave the two Foxes on their own. They were probably drunk somewhere and sleeping it off.

The evening wore on and the sky darkened. The air turned heavier and warmer. Way off, rumbling sounded and streak lightning sliced through the black sky. A storm was moving in. Cougar Woman got on her horse and signaled for the others to do the same. "This is a good time to go," she said. "They will be in their tepees out of the rain, and not looking for us."

They mounted and moved to the gate. No one was around as the rain began pelting down, the thunder growling. Their horses skittered into the open. The darkness and the driving rain hid their identity as they rode back to the bluff. Bolts of lightning showed the way, and soon they were up on the trail heading for shelter, if they could find it, in a cave or under an overhang.

The rain was cool and the air smelled of wet soil and greenery. Quietly, Cougar Woman gave thanks to Mother Earth for her help. Tomorrow she would make an offering of tobacco. Her mind shifted to the trade whiskey; their people should be prevented from getting it. The whiskey would demoralize them and defeat them without a fight. The white people were smart. They knew how to get what they wanted.

Sweet Grass was pleased with his goods, though he was more pleased with a discovery he had made. When he was in the store with the white trader, the man had been touching him while showing him the goods. The feel of the man's hot hand excited him. His people did not stroke one another, even lightly, unless they were making a specific show of affection—or were husband and wife, or brother and sister. It aroused feelings he had not known before.

Cougar Woman was relieved when they got into the mountains. She was also angry with the two Foxes and had made up her mind to talk to Tall Bull about the white man's whiskey. She looked at Sweet Grass fidgeting on his horse and sensed something different about him. She hoped he'd gotten what he wanted from the white man's store. At least Bold Eagle had his capote.

Sweet Grass was very satisfactory as far as she was concerned. He relieved Raven of extra jobs she didn't need. He was quite skilled, and she hoped he didn't regret his chosen role. She patted her horse on the withers. This was a remarkably swift animal. Sweet Grass had told her she would find it in front of a chief's lodge. In fact, it had been a Pecunie chief's best racehorse, and it easily outran her pursuers the day she stole it. It was not surprising the Pecunie chief prized this mare with the star-shaped white mark on its forehead. She relaxed and let her thoughts wander as they drew nearer to camp.

Bold Eagle's shoulder pained him. It throbbed with every step his horse took. He was sure Sweet Grass had tended well to it, though he did not trust that burning liquid the white man applied. Something about the hairy-faced trader bothered him. He smelled bad and his eyes were constantly shifting—never looking directly at you.

He was pleased to get the new capote. It was white with wide black and red stripes at the bottom. There was a red band around the hood where it met his face. He stroked the soft woolly surface. Bold Eagle's thoughts turned to women. He looked at Cougar Woman, comparing her with the girl he had after their last successful raid. The girl—he couldn't remember her name—had been soft like the new capote, pliable, and eager to please. They enjoyed each other. She was round where women should be, he thought, not hard and angular like Cougar Woman.

He jerked his mind away from thoughts unworthy of him and of Cougar Woman. She was his brother—not a woman he would want to lie with. As for Swift Water Woman, his wife, she was good around the tepee but he was so used to her that he rarely thought of her unless out of necessity.

Sweet Grass he viewed with some pity, as he had no interest in women. Bold Eagle could not understand this, although if The One Above planned it that way, it must be all right. There was room enough for differences.

He smelled wood smoke on the wind as they came into a broad valley. Camp was close by. He would tell Tall Bull about Cougar Woman's courage. She was very brave and he was sorry he could not have helped her. He thought of the two drunken Foxes. He had been a Fox ever since they invited him to take his father's place, and he was ashamed of those two. Each should be asked to "carry the staff" on the next raid to make up for his cowardice at the trading post.

Bold Eagle looked over at his little brother riding beside him. He was a good boy, a good warrior. Bold Eagle felt protective. He motioned to Crooked Nose, and the boy came closer. "I am riding ahead to tell Tall Bull of his daughter's bravery. You stay with her." He urged his horse to a gallop, gritting his teeth against the pain, to be sure the criers would spread the word about Cougar Woman.

When Tall Bull heard hoofbeats stopping in front of his tepee, he rushed outside. Bold Eagle was already off his horse.

"Tall Bull, I have just come from the white man's trading post. Cougar Woman attacked and killed three Pecunies with no help from two cowardly Foxes." Disgust showed on his face. "She counted coup against one and brought back two of their bows. I was wounded and she avenged me."

Tall Bull had conflicting emotions, but his pride in Cougar Woman's achievement won over his shame at the behavior of the two Foxes and his disappointment that she and Bold Eagle had gone to the post against his wishes. "Tell me in detail what happened," he requested. Then turning to Raven, he said, "Get the criers. This must be told to all."

Bold Eagle told him everything. He explained how quickly it was over and how Cougar Woman had attacked with cunning and prowess. "She should be a war leader," he concluded. "She has made coups and proved her courage."

When Raven appeared with the criers, Tall Bull told them, and they began their course through the village crying loudly to everyone the tale of Cougar Woman's accomplishments. That night there would be celebrating in her honor, and the story would be recounted many times by those who had been there.

Just after the criers left, Cougar Woman rode up. She dismounted and Tall Bull embraced her. "I have heard from Bold Eagle," he said, his voice thick with pride. "You have made me very pleased."

She felt her throat tighten with emotion, but kept her face immobile.

Raven smiled at her lovingly and patted her shoulder. Then people began to praise her loudly, calling her "chief." She began to feel slightly important. She caught sight of Running Fox's face in the crowd. He sneered at her, and she realized he was an enemy who would stop at nothing to humiliate her. She knew she must never feel too secure with her power.

Early one morning, Cougar Woman set out for the Mountain of the Cougars. She took her weapons, her robe, and some pemmican. As she rode up the trail behind the village, she turned to look at the rows of tepees glowing in the morning light. Spirals of smoke came from fires burning inside, and the smell of wood smoke was on the air. Birds greeted the dawn with song. Somewhere close by a mountain bluebird warbled.

At the base of the mountain trail she turned her horse loose and climbed ahead on foot. The rushing stream beside the trail drowned out most sounds. She left the trail at the place where she remembered Sweet Grass had spent his time when they had all come for their first quest. Soon she found a green meadow. There were rock walls on the peak side and many blueberry bushes. She walked along picking berries to eat yet remembering her mission. She came upon a small lake with a herd of elk grazing nearby. Something made her turn around, whereupon she saw two grizzlies following her trail. She fitted an arrow to her bow and kept walking, wondering if they were after her or just looking for berries. She thought if she killed a grizzly she could eat the heart and its courage would always be hers. With her mind made up, she turned to face the bears. When they saw her stop, one of them reared up on its hind legs, opening its arms like a lover.

"Help me, honored one," she said. "Make my arrow fly straight." In her heart she heard her answer.

The bear came nearer and she aimed carefully, sending the arrow toward its massive chest. As the feathered shaft buried itself in the bear's fur, a thunderous roar of pain and rage split the silence and reverberated off the cliffs. Cougar Woman shot another arrow, and the huge beast came at her in a fury of claws, but it fell before it reached her, its eyes glazed with death. The other bear, witnessing the sudden killing of its companion, turned unexpectedly and lumbered back up the trail.

"Forgive me for killing you," she said to the spirit of the slain bear. "You shall go with me, because you are braver than any other creature on earth." She skinned the bear and, taking its great warm heart in her hands, drank some of its blood. She could feel new strength flooding through her. Then she continued her climb.

Finally she came to an open spot that felt right to her. She put down her robe and the grizzly skin and heart. Taking her cougar medicine bundle, she opened it and threw some of the powdered heart in the four directions. She prayed to The One Above to send her spirit helper to her again. Afterward, she sat back and listened to the wind scream around the peak. She soon fell asleep.

The first thing she knew of was a warm, rough tongue licking her face. She opened her eyes and looked directly into the firecoal eyes of a cougar.

Wake up. I have a message for you.

She sat up and faced the cougar. Pointing to the bearskin and heart, she said, "I have brought you the heart of a grizzly."

The cat walked over, sniffed it, and turned back to her, twitching its great tail. *We shall eat the grizzly heart together. You eat a quarter of it and I will eat the rest. It will help you be strong. Divide the heart.*

She did as the cougar told her and they both ate. Then the cougar lay licking its chops and cleaning its paws. Cougar Woman waited. Everything was quiet; even the wind had stopped.

You have done well, Cougar Woman. You are known as a very brave warrior—one who is not afraid of anything. Like all leaders, you have many enemies, too. Your reputation is spreading across the plains. Even the Dakotah have heard of Cougar Woman of the Absaroke. You will lead many war parties. One will transport you far away to the land of the "people who take heads." There you will find horses and save your friends. You will also take a trip to the south, where you will see strange sights.

She looked up at the bright blue sky with puffy wind clouds and saw a queer square object floating there. It was piled on other squares, and small dark people in colorful clothing were climbing ladders and disappearing into the squares.

I see much fighting; you will learn from your trips. Now I must go. Take the grizzly skin and make it into leggings. Pray to Mother Earth and Father Sky, Cougar Woman. Do it every day you are in this world. The cougar got up and stretched, then bounded behind some rocks and vanished.

Cougar Woman sat for a few minutes thinking about the message her spirit helper had given her. Then she got up and, taking her medicine bundle as well as the grizzly skin and her robe, started down the mountain wondering why she would be going to the land of the Dakotah.

The Dakotah

BOLD EAGLE AND COUGAR WOMAN CAME BACK TO EMPTY TEPEES following an afternoon hunt. She was the first to discover something wrong. The fire that Raven always had going was cold. She knew Tall Bull had spent most of the day in council with Weasel Bear and several of the other old honored men. She was worried.

Then Bold Eagle appeared. "Swift Water Woman is gone. I cannot find her. No one has seen her since this morning when several women went berrying." He was visibly upset.

Cougar Woman looked carefully around the tepee. "Raven and Sweet Grass must have gone berrying as well," she concluded. "Their baskets are gone. Let's find them."

They rode away from the village, following the river toward the east. There was a favorite berrying patch about a mile away where the chokecherries that were much prized dry as winter food grew lush and full. Cougar Woman galloped to the patch, with Bold Eagle right behind her. They were greeted with silence—no laughing women enjoying their berrying.

As she dismounted, something caught her eye. On the other side of a clump of bushes, Absaroke baskets lay over-turned, gathered berries covered the ground, and everything had been trampled upon. Then she heard a moan. She moved cautiously, fearing a trap. Parting a thick clump of chokecher-ries, she found Raven lying on her face.

Cougar Woman eased Raven over and her eyes opened. There was a superficial wound on her head where she'd been grazed by an arrow, but aside from that, she had no injuries.

"You will be all right, mother," Cougar Woman tried to reassure her. She sensed Raven was still very frightened.

She helped Raven to her horse, then she and Bold Eagle rode back to the village, where they put Raven on her bed. Cougar Woman bathed her wound and put a poultice on it to ease the pain. Then she, Bold Eagle, and Tall Bull sat while Raven told them her story.

"Six of us went to gather berries. We did not think there would be enemies about. We were having such fun. Sweet Grass was singing to us and we were all laughing. Swift Water Woman was happiest of all. She was to have a child when the geese come again."

Bold Eagle felt the hatred for his enemies swell in his heart.

"As we filled our baskets, suddenly everything around us grew silent. Even the birds stopped singing. We felt fearful and were starting home when they appeared. I screamed and ran back to the bushes. I felt a piercing pain on the side of my head and fell. I crawled deeper into the thicket and lay still; I dared not breathe. They did not look for me."

Cougar Woman was glad Raven was safe but wondered about Sweet Grass and Bold Eagle's woman. She felt great sadness for her brother. They shall pay, she thought. "Which enemy was it, Raven? The Striped Feathered Arrows, the Poor Lodges, the Snakes? Or was it . . . the Dakotah?" The hate gorged up in her as she remembered long years ago.

Raven answered, weeping, "Dakotah—they took them all."

Tall Bull listened, thankful the spirits had seen fit to return Raven to him. Now Cougar Woman and Bold Eagle would go to the land of the Dakotah to bring back the berry pickers. He took his ceremonial pipe from the tepee pole where he kept it, and handed it to Cougar Woman. "Take my pipe and lead a war party. Bring back the captives."

She took the long pipe and looked at it. It was the one she always admired, with its intricately carved red stone bowl and bright feathered decorations. "I shall carry the pipe, father," she said. "We will go after the hated Dakotah and bring back many scalps. Bold Eagle will be a Wolf." She wondered if it was a wise choice but decided he would not be overly eager because it might endanger Swift Water Woman, and besides Cougar Woman knew she could trust him above all others.

Word went out to the Foxes that a party would go after the Dakotah. Twenty warriors volunteered to go. Running Fox's woman, Buffalo Calf, and Crooked Nose's mother, Morning, were among those who had been taken, so these men would go too. Cougar Woman was not pleased at having Running Fox in her party, but she sympathized with him. Most of the warriors were glad Cougar Woman would carry the pipe and lead the group. They respected her and knew she would see that they brought back many scalps.

They picked up the trail and headed east, crossing the Big Horn River and skirting the peaks. Although Cougar Woman sent Wolves ahead, they did not catch sight of the Dakotah, who'd had several days' head start. They camped at night beside the Powder River, named for the fine dust that horses kicked up along its banks. They were careful to conceal their camp in brush and to avoid making fires. They were close to Dakotah territory, and Cougar Woman did not want to endanger the war party or the captives.

Bold Eagle came in late at night. He was plastered with

mud and had tiny mud ears on his head. He sat beside Cougar Woman, eating while he told her what he had learned.

"Many days ahead there is a large village. It sits beneath a strange stone stump in a green valley beside a river. The great stone rises toward Father Sky and can be seen from a long distance away. It is almost as high as our peaks but is flattened on top."

"How large is their village?"

"Many lodges—one hundred. Not so great as the buffalo herd." Bold Eagle smiled. "It is about the size of our own."

"Did you see signs of the prisoners?"

"No. Perhaps they are not there."

"Go again and take the other Wolves with you. Look carefully and find out where our people are."

Bold Eagle rolled up to sleep a few hours. Shortly before dawn he was gone.

The war party rode that day, being careful to watch for signs of the enemy. They camped again in a sheltered glade and posted guards. The Wolves had not reappeared—a sign that they had found the captured ones, Cougar Woman hoped.

Late that night, Bold Eagle returned with one other Wolf. "We have looked their camp over thoroughly and the captives are not there," he said. "Perhaps they took them toward the black hills."

Cougar Woman considered this. They had followed the trail of the Dakotah war party and it had led here. If the captives were not here, they might have gone on to the country of the hills with the black trees, as Bold Eagle suggested. She would have to follow, but the trail would be hazardous. "We will follow, but at night we will pass the Dakotah village at the foot of the earth tower. We do not want to fight until we find those we are searching for."

Word was passed to the warriors, who were in agreement. They would follow the trail of the captives.

Bold Eagle and the Wolves went ahead, and on the other

side of the big village picked up a well-used trail leading toward the sunrise. The next day Cougar Woman led her warriors within sight of the earth tower. Then they cut south and rested until nightfall. They could see the huge tower silhouetted in the moonlight, and smell the smoke from the Dakotah fires, and hear drifting on the breeze the usual camp sounds of dogs and people. They stole around the village. On the other side, they rode east until daybreak, when Bold Eagle returned. This time he was pleased.

He reported to Cougar Woman: "We have found them with a war party camped a day's ride from here. The party is going to their village but we do not know how far it is."

"How many warriors?"

"Only twelve."

She signaled the Absaroke riders to come closer and told them of Bold Eagle's findings. "We will surround and attack their camp at night and kill them all."

Bold Eagle went ahead. The main party following him soon came to the trail of the Dakotah. Very little was said when they stopped to prepare for battle.

Cougar Woman took her medicine and spread it on the ground before her. She applied lightning streaks of vermilion paint to her cheeks and forehead. She rubbed on her cougar medicine and prayed for help. Then she put on her cougar shirt and tied her medicine bundle back on her belt.

After a council with the warriors, she sent Running Fox ahead with one third of the group to get around the Dakotah and cut them off. She had Crooked Nose go to keep an eye on him, although Running Fox, she knew, was eager to retrieve his woman and therefore willing to cooperate. She led the rest of the war party.

Bold Eagle gave wolf howls, which were answered by two of their Wolves ahead of the Dakotah. "They are camped by a stream not far away," he told Cougar Woman. "They do not suspect we are after them in their own country."

"Good." She urged her horse along the trail and the others followed. Bold Eagle went ahead. The next time he howled, Cougar Woman stopped and dismounted. The rest followed and, taking their war clubs and other weapons, sneaked on foot to within sight of the Dakotah.

Cougar Woman saw Sweet Grass lying on the ground with the other captives nearby. Swift Water Woman seemed to be giving him something to drink. The Dakotah warriors were not paying attention to the captives. They were sitting around the fire eating and laughing, at ease in their own territory. Two of them were gambling. The presence of enemies was far from their minds. She signaled her party to fan out.

No sound was heard as they crawled close to the campfire circle. Cougar Woman gave a hoot of an owl and was answered by Running Fox on the other side of the Dakotah camp. She hooted again and gave the Absaroke war cry. The Dakotah were attacked before they could get their weapons up. Cougar Woman took the nearest warrior, hitting him on the face with her coup stick, then swinging her war club into the side of his head. His dying eyes had a startled look. She turned to the next one, but by now he was dead, as were they all. She and her party scalped the ones they had each killed, then went to tend to the captives. Bold Eagle was already there and Swift Water Woman was beside him.

"They are all fine except for Sweet Grass," he said. "He was badly beaten."

Cougar Woman knelt beside Sweet Grass, who could barely open his eyes. She called several warriors and told them to make a litter so he could be carried on a horse. There was no time to waste, however, for the big Dakotah camp was between them and safety.

Cougar Woman decided to go north, following the stream and cutting to the west well above the Dakotah village. Taking the Dakotah horses and what booty they could find, they rode away. The Wolves went out in front and on both sides as the war party started back. Except for Sweet Grass and Swift Water Woman, who seemed visibly shaken, the captives appeared in good condition.

Cougar Woman rode beside Sweet Grass for a few minutes. "You will be treated when we get out of Dakotah territory," she assured him.

Sweet Grass smiled painfully. "Did Raven get away?" he asked.

"Yes. She is fine. Bold Eagle and I found her. An arrow had wounded her, but that was all."

They rode for days without seeing enemies and moved beyond the earth tower. One afternoon, a Wolf came in and reported a small party of Striped Feathered Arrows heading in their direction. Cougar Woman stopped the group and took the medicine bundle off her belt. She reached for some powdered cougar heart, letting it drift in the breeze. Then she looked for a vision under the cougar skin she had placed on the ground in front of her. There she saw a party of six enemy warriors coming from the south and riding toward the mountains.

Cougar Woman took twelve warriors and directed the rest to continue their homeward journey. "We shall go to collect the scalps of the Striped Feathered Arrows," she said as she galloped away with the painted warriors. She left Bold Eagle behind with one other Wolf.

Her own Wolf went ahead and soon came back to say that the Striped Feathered Arrows were unaware anyone was after them and were camped for the night.

Cougar Woman led the warriors close to the enemy camp. There they dismounted, leaving their horses with Crooked Nose.

Cougar Woman glided like a shadow through cottonwood and willow clumps near the stream. Her warriors spread out and moved as one. The Striped Feathered Arrows were around their campfire. From behind her came a shout. One of her warriors was grappling with an enemy while the rest raced for cover. She fitted an arrow to her bow and shot the man as he stood silhouetted against the firelight. He threw his arms into the air and pitched forward. She could see no one else.

She was unhappy that her Wolf had not discovered the enemy warrior out of camp. Stumbling over him in the dark had ruined their surprise attack.

She hooted twice and crept toward her horse. The hoots sounded all around as the Absaroke party retreated.

Once on her horse, she waited until the rest of the warriors came back. When they were well away from the Striped Feathered Arrows, her people rested.

Running Fox approached Cougar Woman. "You should not be the pipe holder," he said. "You are not fit. No woman is fit for anything but to serve a man's needs."

She looked at him silently for a moment. "Because I told you to slip away and not fight those you could not see?"

"Yes! We should have killed them all."

She turned from him and walked to the fire where the Wolf One Ear was eating. "When you go out," she said, "pick up the trail of the Striped Feathered Arrows. We will kill them and take their horses tomorrow at dawn when we can see what we are doing."

One Ear nodded, pleased by her good sense. Shortly, he got up and left. Cougar Woman had guards surrounding the camp. She wanted to take no chance of failure. After she had slept for a time, One Ear shook her awake. "I have found the Striped Feathered Arrows. They are well guarded now, and sleeping."

She rose and, taking her medicine bundle, threw some powdered cougar heart to the earth and sky, letting it drift on the slight wind. "Help us, Medicine Father," she said. "Let us conquer our enemies, the Striped Feathered Arrows of the north."

The warriors mounted and rode silently toward the enemy camp. This time Cougar Woman left the horses sooner and took five men ahead with her to be sure the enemy guards were silenced. She came up behind one sitting with his back to a cottonwood tree, his head nodding as he struggled to stay awake. She took her knife, carefully balancing it in her hand, and threw it at him. The knife caught him in the throat. He clutched his neck and slumped forward. She bent over him and quickly scalped him. Not a sound was made other than the slight tearing as his scalp left the skull.

She turned and moved in closer to the Striped Feathered Arrow camp. Horses were nickering off to the left. One of the Wolves must be there, she thought, wondering for a fleeting moment what the horses were like. She heard a snapping of brush and froze, waiting—every sense alert. She could smell him and hear him breathe before she could see him. The man appeared in the bushes, squatted, and pulled his loincloth aside. Cougar Woman, knife in hand, moved in. No leaf crackled; no twig broke. Like a ghost she slipped behind him, put her hand over his mouth, and slit his throat in one movement, jumping aside to let his dead body topple over backward. She did not want to scalp him, because his smell was too bad.

The Striped Feathered Arrows around the fire were asleep. Across the campsite she saw movement. Her warriors were there. She gave a soft cry of a night bird and her answer came back. She moved into the open and attacked the nearest Striped Feathered Arrow. Her warriors were beside her and it was over in seconds. They took scalps and rounded up the horses. She noticed that Running Fox was quiet and kept out of her way. She was pleased that no Absaroke had been hurt.

They drove the captured horses before them and caught up with Bold Eagle. When they reached the Powder River, Cougar Woman breathed more easily. They had a small herd of about twenty-five horses, many scalps, and the captives they had come for. But there were still many days of travel before they would be safely away.

As the group continued toward the mountains in the

west, things seemed to go well until one afternoon. Bold
Eagle came to Cougar Woman in alarm. "We are being followed by a large war party and they are gaining on us," he
reported.

She immediately split the group. She sent Bold Eagle
ahead with the former captives on fast horses and some of the
captured ones for spare mounts. Most of the warriors stayed
behind. The Wolves were out and reporting regularly,
although she could already see the dust of the pursuers.

When the Dakotah were close enough to follow them, she
cut south, away from the route Bold Eagle had taken. The
Dakotah, eager to fight and regain their injured pride, trailed
them. Some were firing black sticks they had gotten from the
white man. The crack of the guns reached the fleeing
Absaroke warriors. Heading toward a butte, Cougar Woman
noticed darkness approaching and led her warriors up the
steep sides of the hill.

The Dakotah rode up the butte before they realized the
Absaroke were above them. By then, Absaroke arrows had
claimed several Dakotah warriors. A shot from a Dakotah
caught One Ear between the eyes and he died in a kneeling
position. The sky darkened and Cougar Woman passed the
word that they would leave before first light of morning.

One by one, leading their horses quietly behind, the
Absaroke came off the butte past the Dakotah. Once out of
earshot, they leaped on their horses and rode away.

Cougar Woman's departure was less hasty. Quietly leading her spotted buffalo horse, she passed close enough to a
sleeping Dakotah to steal the horse tethered beside him. Then
she saw the outline of a black stick on the ground and
grabbed it for herself. Bold Eagle, she knew, would show her
how to use it, although she preferred the silent speed of an
arrow.

Cougar Woman and her war party were soon in the Big
Horns climbing up to the alpine meadows and the rich hunt-

ing grounds below Cloud Peak. Snowcaps loomed above them as they made their way deeper into Absaroke country. It was chilly and snow flurries drifted around them. Cougar Woman steeled her body against the discomfort of the gathering cold. She concentrated on thoughts that she had brought the captives safely home and had lost only one warrior—unless Bold Eagle, who was to meet them in less than a day's ride, had gotten into trouble. She did not know how many scalps had been taken. She had three and a warrior's horse. She inhaled deeply and caught the smell of smoke. Signaling to Running Fox, she stopped.

Running Fox rode up beside her. He waited with an impassive face for her directions, grudgingly respecting her abilities but never forgiving her for being a woman. His dark eyes were venomous.

"There is a camp somewhere nearby. Ride out in One Ear's place and find where the smoke comes from," she told him.

Without replying, Running Fox wheeled his spotted pony and galloped out of sight. Cougar Woman sat on her horse, gazing after him. The rest of the warriors waited for their leader's signal as they, too, smelled the smoke, which carried the scent of cooking meat. They were tired and would welcome warm food in their bellies.

Cougar Woman reflected on Running Fox. He was causing no trouble, but she knew she must never trust him. His eyes were like a snake's, ready to strike. She put him out of her mind and looked at her band of warriors. Their horses were standing quietly. Steam was coming out of their nostrils. Occasionally a horse shuffled and snorted, but that was the only sound other than the moaning of the wind.

She heard hoofbeats—two horses were coming their way. She signaled the warriors to be ready. Then she saw Bold Eagle and Running Fox racing toward them. She kicked her horse and rode out to greet them.

As they pulled into the small camp Bold Eagle had set up, the warriors were excited. An elk had been killed and the women were cooking it. Several men went out and soon returned with more elk to add to the feast. Others set up additional brush shelters in case the snow flurries turned into a fall snowstorm. Guards were posted and the small band ate and rested.

Cougar Woman took her medicine bundle and walked a few hundred yards from camp to a point where she could look up at the swirling grayness of Cloud Peak. She opened her bundle in a sheltered spot beneath a grove of aspen trees whose fallen leaves lay golden on the ground. Taking some powdered heart, she let it drift with the breeze and mix with the flurries. Then she looked up at the peak and prayed to her spirit helper and to her Father, the Sky, and her Mother, the Earth. She gave thanks for their protection. She also took a small star-shaped rock from her bundle and offered it to the spirit of One Ear—a brave and loyal warrior whose body they had to leave behind.

As if in answer to her prayers, a ray of sunlight flooded the green meadow before her and everything in its path shimmered in gold. While she stood gazing at the beauty of the land, a cougar emerged from a stand of aspens and bathed in the golden light for a moment before bounding away.

Cougar Woman folded up her medicine bundle and strode back to camp. Her body was heavy with fatigue and she would sleep peacefully, knowing her cougar helper was nearby.

It took three more days to find the band of Tall Bull on its move toward the buffalo plains for the fall hunt. The war party first saw the long line of animals and people from a rise—it looked like an elongated caterpillar crawling along an ancient trail.

Cougar Woman stopped and sent word that they would follow the flanks of Tall Bull's band until evening, when his people camped for the night. Then they would ride in and put on a show for everyone.

Meanwhile, all the warriors dressed in their best finery. Cougar Woman wore an eagle feather warbonnet she carried in a case strapped to her saddle and held her new rifle and shield with the painted cougar. Bold Eagle, beside her, also wore a warbonnet; his black hair, now loose from its bindings, trailed over his horse's rump. Swift Water Woman, proud of this handsome and bold fighter, rode beside him carrying his shield and trying to hide the pain she was feeling. They pranced their horses along, riding the fringes of Tall Bull's caravan, far enough away so that the people were not aware of them.

A Wolf came to Cougar Woman. "Tall Bull sends greetings to his daughter—Cougar Woman, chief of the Absaroke. He welcomes you home. He is glad you will be here to hunt buffalo with him again."

"Tell Tall Bull, my father, that I am glad to be back and will bring the war party in when his camp is made."

The scout rode back with the news and several hours later the war party galloped their horses down the rolling hills to the camp.

They yelled and whooped their delight at being home. Everyone came out, clapped, and shouted praises. Cougar Woman at the head cavorted her spotted horse around, showing off her riding skills. Her eagle feathers streamed behind as she raced him straight at a tepee, hauling him up or changing direction at top speed. Many women tried to steal the scalps she had tied to the gun, but she managed to elude their grasping hands.

When the excitement died down, she threw herself off her horse and embraced her father. Raven, looking like her old self, stood beside him with welcome in her dark eyes. She was also glad to see Sweet Grass.

Cougar Woman pleased Tall Bull with the horse she had taken from the sleeping Dakotah, and they went into the tepee to sit and smoke. Tonight she would tell what they had done, and the others would listen and add their own versions of the story. Women would dance with the scalps. She had already given Raven three. Now as she sat and puffed on the ceremonial pipe with Tall Bull, Cougar Woman wondered what she would do after the hunt. Tall Bull wasted no time telling her.

"The white man's government is sending a commission to the northern trading people, the Lodges at the Extreme End, near our relatives the Earth Lodges on the Big River. Weasel Bear and I have been invited to represent our people and come to an understanding with the whites.

"That is not possible." Cougar Woman spat out the words, thinking of the hairy-faced one and the whiskey he gave so freely.

"I agree, but it is always wise to learn about your enemies. I shall go and I want you to go with me."

She nodded. She would do whatever Tall Bull asked although the white man, she knew, was treacherous. She was sure Tall Bull did not trust them either, but she wondered about the others. "Where does Weasel Bear stand?" she asked.

"He is for peace with the whites. Some of our people claim the whites are driving out the Indian nations, pushing them farther and farther away from their ancestral lands and closer to our mountains. If the white men continue to push us all and we go beyond the mountains, we shall eventually find the Great Waters. Then where do we go?" Tall Bull paused as if pondering this question.

"Weasel Bear thinks that if we stay friends with the whites, we may keep our lands. I do not agree, but will hold my counsel," he added.

"Bold Eagle shares that view," said Cougar Woman. "Perhaps it is the right one, but I do not think friendship will stop the white men if they want our lands. They are too greedy for that. They have trapped so many beaver in the eastern country that the streams are empty. They will do the same here."

"It is sad." Tall Bull puffed on his pipe, holding its long stem in his hand. "Maybe we will get a better idea of what we face when we meet with them in the next green grass time."

"Yes. Let us not waste pleasant moments talking of them." She sat back and closed her eyes, reflecting on the goodness of their lives and the coming hunt. They would take many buffalo to keep them comfortable through the winter. She hoped the spirits would guide them well.

Part III

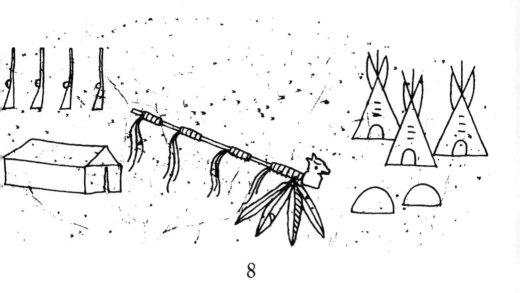

8

Tall Bull

THE BERRIES WERE RIPE AND THE YOUNG GEESE IN THE SHALLOW
sections of the rivers and lakes were trying their wings. It was
almost midsummer when Tall Bull gave the order to journey
to the lands of the Lodges at the Extreme End. Some of the
band—the older ones, the very young, and the pregnant
women—would stay with their cousins the Many Lodges
while Tall Bull would go as part of a delegation to meet with
commissioners from the government of the white man. At his
side he wanted Cougar Woman as well as Bold Eagle, who
was interested in terms with the whites. Tall Bull deemed it
wise to listen to both sides.

Chief Weasel Bear and a delegation from his band also
went, and the two groups were to meet along the Elk River
not far from where it joined the Big. The buffalo were plentiful, and as Tall Bull rode across the open grasslands he
watched vast numbers of shaggy beasts while they lumbered
away from the riders. He wondered about Cougar Woman's
vision of long ago as well as his own prophetic dreams.

Would the buffalo be wiped out? If so, there would be no way for his people to survive. He looked at the line behind him. Many of his people were coming to the meeting. His warriors rode on the flanks. They were a brave and handsome lot, these people of his. He sat even straighter and fondled the pipe he carried on one hand. He didn't change his expression as his horse sidestepped a prairie dog hole and stumbled. Tall Bull remained deep in thought, his eyes squinted, his brow furrowed. The irate prairie dog chattered loudly and disappeared down its passageway. There was a large dogtown here, and the Absaroke were riding along its edges, enduring the scolding barks of little "wish-ton-a-wish," the prairie dog people.

Cougar Woman and Bold Eagle rode behind him, their eyes searching the horizon for signs of humans other than themselves. The prairie dogs amused Cougar Woman. To her, they were like a group of women washing at the river or dressing hides together, talking all the time. Their entire community was one of coming and going. Bold Eagle ignored them; he was thinking about the loss of his baby, who would have been born by now if all had gone well.

Suddenly Tall Bull's Wolves came in and reported. Then Tall Bull held up his arm to halt the line. Bold Eagle and Cougar Woman moved closer to listen.

"The band of Weasel Bear waits around the next bend. They have set up camp. Beyond that there is no sign of anyone."

Tall Bull nodded his head. His long hair streamed out behind him, blowing in the brisk breeze as he sat listening to the reporting scouts. His horse, a black and white buffalo pony Cougar Woman had given him, stood motionless, its long mane and tail billowing out like Tall Bull's hair.

Tall Bull raised his scalp-bedecked arm again and, in a sweeping motion, pointed ahead. His horse began moving and the line followed. He thought about Weasel Bear, who was waiting for him. Since boyhood, they had been friends.

When their two bands got together, their parents often pitched lodges beside each other and enjoyed one another's company. Weasel Bear had become a bold warrior, even bolder than Tall Bull. As such, he was head chief, a wise man; but Weasel Bear, like himself, was getting on in years, the snows of age gathering on his head. Soon it would be time for them to go to the Spirit World. He hoped that before that time they would be wise enough to know what to do with the white man. Tall Bull did not fool himself into believing the white man was honorable.

Weasel Bear rode out to meet them. Behind him several of his bravest chiefs and warriors rode in a line, their warbonnets waving in the wind, their shields and lances in their hands. They made a fine sight galloping over the hill and hollering greetings.

Cougar Woman, Bold Eagle, and four other Foxes rode behind Tall Bull. They, too, looked impressive as they made their fine horses dance around to show off.

Tall Bull was first to speak when the two chiefs came abreast. "Welcome, Weasel Bear. I hope you have not been waiting long."

"No." Weasel Bear, although older than Tall Bull, was not as large and gave the impression of being an old man. "We came to this place yesterday. My men have been hunting so we could feast tonight and talk about our coming visit with the white men."

"Good. We will enjoy that. Your warriors will want to know my chiefs." As he pointed them out—a needless gesture since Weasel Bear knew them all—he said something about their bravery. Weasel Bear did the same with his. Once the formalities were over, they moved along together to the campsite where they put up their lodges. Tall Bull had Raven set theirs in the center of the circle near Weasel Bear's.

That night they feasted as the aroma of cooking meat mingled with smoke from buffalo chip fires. The two band chiefs sat in Weasel Bear's tepee. Behind them in a circle sat their warrior chiefs. The ceremonial pipe was filled, lit, and passed slowly around the circle, each warrior taking a deep draw and exhaling smoke toward the hole in the tepee top. They were in no hurry, each savoring the importance of the moment. Cougar Woman sat directly behind Tall Bull, and when it came time for her to smoke, she held the pipe in her hand and slowly inhaled. The smoke was sharp on her tongue and, as she blew it out, she silently hoped that The One Above would help them in their dealings with the whites.

Tall Bull was first to break the silence. "We are going to meet the white man, and we can be sure he is after one thing—our lands. Since our forefathers came from the east to these high mountains and green valleys, we have honored our lands. Many enemies have tried to take them from us, but our young men have been brave and have fought for what is theirs." Tall Bull paused, then continued. "We have heard much about the white men. We have heard how they have pushed eastern tribes out of their lands. They cheat them, make them drunk, or throw them into stockades like captured animals. There is no justice for our brothers. It is folly to believe the white tide will stop and be satisfied with what it has stolen already. Soon even those who think they are safe will be pursued again like the wolf before the hunter."

Everyone around the circle nodded in agreement. There was no sound but the crackling of the fire and the soughing of the night wind on the plains. Tall Bull went on, his deep voice heavy with sorrow.

"We meet with the white people for the first time. I know what they want. Their trappers are already in our lands, killing our beaver and other animals. Unlike the Pecunies, we have not declared war against the white trapper. But I do not favor giving up our lands."

Tall Bull was silent and Weasel Bear began to speak. His

voice was reedy and old sounding as it penetrated the silence in the tepee.

"Yes, we all know what the white man wants, but we do not know how he means to go about getting it. We now go to meet with him and listen to what he has to say. I do not think fighting the white man is the way. His numbers are like leaves in the forest. When one falls, another takes its place. I think if we make peace with the white man, we will save our lands."

"Do you think," asked Tall Bull, "that the white man's word is good? It has never been good in the past or the eastern tribes—those who are still alive—would not be fleeing."

"I do not know. I only wish to save our people and our lands." Weasel Bear sat down looking wizened beside Tall Bull.

Cougar Woman listened gravely. She was not certain which side was best. The white man's forces were superior, but no white man could fight as well as an Absaroke warrior. Bold Eagle, beside her, was silent. She knew he favored the side of Weasel Bear. The only white man she knew he would have killed was the trapper who had attacked her on their way back from Nez Percé country.

The following morning they broke camp and continued along the Elk River. It would be many days before they reached the villages of the Lodges at the Extreme End. Cougar Woman was eager to see these people who lived in huge round houses covered with earth. Their villages, she knew, were great trading centers beside the Big River. Tribes from all over the north went there to barter for goods.

Known to the Absaroke as the Lodges at the Extreme End—because of their proximity to the Absaroke relatives the Earth Lodges—they were known to most other tribes as the People of the Pheasants. They had two villages, and the first one the Absaroke came to was the main village. Set on a bluff forty feet above the Big River, it had a protective stockade surrounded by plains, some cultivated with crops, rolling away in green hills. As the Absaroke came over a hill, they saw the many permanent earth dwellings clustered like giant toadstools behind the stockade. There were hundreds, Cougar Woman thought, as she looked at the brown domes. And people seemed to be everywhere. A group of dignitaries was riding toward them. Tall Bull and Weasel Bear stopped their horses and waited side-by-side with their warriors lined up behind them.

The head chief rode up to the two Absaroke chiefs, extending his arm in greeting. "Welcome to the home of the People of the Pheasants. I am White Wolf Cub," he said. His voice boomed loud enough to be heard all along the line.

Cougar Woman, intrigued by his elegance, gazed first at his huge raven-feathered headdress blowing in the wind, and then at the rest of his attire. He had a stripe of white paint running above his dark brows and along the bridge of his nose where he had put a large daub on the tip. His costume was colorfully decorated with porcupine quills in every possible place, and scalps of his enemies hung from his long overshirt and the sides of his leggings. His beaded moccasins were fringed with fox fur, and foxtails hung on each heel. A great grizzly bear-claw necklace hung around his neck and reached to his waist. In his hand he held a shield decorated with a brilliant red sun and a lance with many eagle plumes flying near its point.

The man next to him also extended greetings. He was not nearly so richly dressed as White Wolf Cub, but still was obviously a man of importance. "I am Six Bears, second chief of the People of the Pheasants," he announced. "Welcome to the lodges of our people." He pointed to a large flat grassy spot near the entrance to the village. "Pitch your camp there. Tonight we shall feast and get acquainted. Tomorrow there will be games and celebrations for all."

"The white men from the Great White Father have not yet arrived," White Wolf Cub added. "Our scouts have seen them two days down the river. We will enjoy our wait. You will join me for food in my tepee at sunset."

Tall Bull spoke first. "We thank the People of the Pheasants. It has been a long journey from our mountains to your rich green land. We are looking forward to our friendship with you."

Weasel Bear followed. "Our people will set up their tepees. We have brought horses and presents." Weasel Bear gestured toward the horse herd they had brought. The finest two would go to the chiefs.

As the two host chiefs of the People of the Pheasants rode back to their lodges, Tall Bull and Weasel Bear led their people to the designated campsite. Raven and Sweet Grass set up their tepee in the heart of a crescent facing the host village; Weasel Bear's women set theirs up beside it.

The two Absaroke chiefs put on their finest outfits—beautifully decorated shirts with quillwork running down the sleeves and across the shoulders in a wide band. The fronts and backs were also colorfully decorated and fringed. Wearing their long feathered warbonnets and carrying their pipes, they went to the dwelling of the first host chief. Cougar Woman and Bold Eagle went with Tall Bull, and a warrior known as Two Suns went with Weasel Bear. A messenger from White Wolf Cub led the way.

As they walked through the stockade entrance, the five visitors were struck by the size of the earth lodges. People cheered and clapped a welcome. Some were perched on the domelike earth roofs along with buffalo skulls, scalp poles, and skin boats that were used on the river.

The guests walked along corridors between the lodges and eventually came to the open square in the center of the village. The chief's lodge faced the square. White Wolf Cub stood in the doorway of his lodge waiting for them.

Once inside the lodge, Cougar Woman was amazed at the many luxuries this chief enjoyed. The interior was at least sixty feet in diameter. A crackling fire burned in the central fire pit and the smell of cooking meat wafted across the room. Along the walls were sleeping compartments for the chief, his various women, and the children. These could be made private by dropping the decorated skins that hung on the walls. Between the alcoves hung shaggy buffalo head masks used in the buffalo dance. The dirt floors, packed and polished, glistened in the firelight.

The chief indicated where they should sit on the furs and robes provided, and signaled for his women to begin serving the meal. First, he took a rib and heaved it into the fire as an offering of thanks. Then he sat quietly and watched his guests eat.

When the wooden bowl of buffalo ribs came, Cougar Woman smelled the wild sage seasoning on them. She was famished and ate hungrily. A second bowl was passed containing wild turnip pudding with currants. Another bowl was filled to overflowing with pemmican and marrow fat. While his guests ate, White Wolf Cub took out his tobacco and filled his pipe. He shaved off a piece of beaver castor for flavoring and sprinkled some dried buffalo dung on top. Settling back in his furs, he lit it.

Cougar Woman licked her fingers and felt the chief's women watching her curiously. Some silently served the food while others sat waiting for their master to direct them. After the meal, more pipes were lit until Tall Bull broke the silence.

"This is a very fine feast. We thank you. Perhaps you will visit us some day and be *our* guests."

White Wolf Cub nodded. He motioned for the women to come closer. "Now you are my guests and may select one of our young women to seek comfort with tonight."

Cougar Woman noticed Two Suns sitting up and looking at the women as White Wolf Cub spoke.

Weasel Bear answered, "I am too old to enjoy women as I used to. I have much on my mind as well, which is not conducive to lovemaking. Perhaps my son, a brave warrior and chief in his own right, would enjoy this type of frolic."

White Wolf Cub signaled to Two Suns. "You may select a woman who would please you. I have many, as you can see, and not all of them are kept busy by me. They will enjoy sport with a younger man."

Two Suns pointed to a young woman. To Cougar Woman she looked barely old enough for her womanhood. Her hair was light, her eyes blue, and her features finely chiseled. Looking at the visitors, she had the startled expression of a flushed hare. She went obediently to Two Suns, who began fondling her breasts as soon as she sat beside him.

White Wolf Cub addressed Tall Bull. "Do you desire a woman or do you, too, wish to let one of your warriors use her?"

"I have a woman waiting in my lodge. I do not seek change. Perhaps Bold Eagle wishes to choose."

Cougar Woman watched Bold Eagle's expression. He could refuse but he would not. The chief's women were very pretty. Bold Eagle, she knew, was not faithful to his wife.

"I would like the third one," Bold Eagle said, rising and going to her. She took his hand and led him to an alcove. The skin dropped, closing them off from the rest of the group.

Then Two Suns got up with his woman. They, too, went to an alcove and disappeared from view. Cougar Woman smoked her pipe and waited for White Wolf Cub's next move. Perhaps he would offer her a woman as well.

"I have had word that the white men will be here tomorrow when the sun sets. We will meet with them outside the stockade."

"We will be ready," said Tall Bull. "Will our cousins the People of the Earth Lodges come as well?"

"Their chief, Black Moccasin, leaves to join us tomorrow. He will then see his kin from the mountains. It is the time of their corn harvest and much celebrating is going on."

"We shall ride with him to his village before we return," Tall Bull offered, ignoring White Wolf Cub's glances at

Cougar Woman. He decided that the man did not know what to offer her. She seemed oblivious as she puffed on her pipe.

Weasel Bear stood up to leave. Tall Bull and Cougar Woman followed. The two warriors would finish their pleasures and return when they pleased.

"Tomorrow we will have games when the sun is directly overhead," White Wolf Cub explained. "Your warriors shall compete with mine."

Weasel Bear nodded his acceptance of the challenge and walked out of the lodge. It had been a good night.

The next day as they led their horses to the race ground, Cougar Woman couldn't resist a dig at Bold Eagle. "Did White Wolf Cub's woman give you pleasure? She was a pretty girl but not very old."

Bold Eagle had enjoyed her innocence. "She was young and untried. White Wolf Cub had not slept with the girl. Perhaps she was a new wife, or he is an old man and needs someone to break them in for him." He smiled at the memory.

"You'd better stay away from her tonight. He won't offer her again if he knows what is good for him," Cougar Woman said, laughing.

Bold Eagle laughed back. "She liked it well enough when I rammed her like a bull. She'll make a good wife after she learns a few tricks."

They had come to an open area where the grass was short from past races. The wild game had been driven away, although pheasants and other birds flew all around them. Already a crowd had gathered and several People of the Pheasants were there with racehorses.

"So far I've seen nothing that will give this horse much competition," Cougar Woman said to Bold Eagle as she surveyed the field.

"Only mine," he retorted as he danced his Nez Percé horse around.

"Let's save our speed for the People of the Pheasants."

White Wolf Cub and his second chief arrived with their wives to watch and scream for their own. Several were already laying bets on favorite horses.

Tall Bull greeted White Wolf Cub and Six Bears. "I have two warriors here to race your best." He pointed to Cougar Woman and Bold Eagle. "Shall we have two races? If we have winners from each, we can race a final time tomorrow." The host chiefs agreed and signaled two warriors to ride up beside them.

One was a small man, heavily painted and riding a black and white. The other was on a roan that looked ungainly with a big body and tiny pipestem legs. The People of the Pheasants cheered their two champions while the visiting Absaroke hissed displeasure.

Cougar Woman pranced her Pecunie mare to the starting line. The opposing roan came up beside her. Six Bears stood where he could see both riders. He pointed to a finish line about a mile away. The course was flat and hard packed from many races. He raised his lance and brought it down hard— the race was on.

Cougar Woman kicked her mare and shot away like an arrow, stretching her legs so that every stride felt like she was flying. The roan kept up beside her, running hard, its rider crouched over its neck, whipping it with a quirt for all he was worth.

Cougar Woman yelled to her mare—"Fly! Fly!"—and the horse, seeming to sense the urgency, increased its speed. Soon the roan dropped back and the mare flew along, adding more distance until it crossed the finish line to a cheering, waving crowd. Cougar Woman pulled in her horse and cantered up to Tall Bull, who smiled his approval.

He signaled Bold Eagle on his spotted horse to go to the starting line. His opponent was already there on his dancing paint. Six Bears raised the lance. It fell, and Bold Eagle's horse lagged at the start. He ran behind the fast little paint until

Bold Eagle used his quirt. Then the big spotted animal, knowing what was wanted of him, put on speed and gradually
gained on the paint. They ran neck and neck to the finish. At
the last minute Bold Eagle's horse surged ahead and won by
a nose. Everyone hollered. They loved to see good horses run.

White Wolf Cub was impressed. Tall Bull led a fine Nez
Percé buffalo horse to him and presented it as a gift. He was
delighted, since this type of horse was rare in his part of the
plains.

All afternoon they raced and feasted and played compet-
itive games. Groups went to the river and frolicked in the
water. It was hot. The sun beat down and the cool water felt
good.

Tall Bull and Weasel Bear sat in sage-scented steam in a
sweat lodge until beads of perspiration poured off of them.
Afterward they plunged into the river.

Cougar Woman and Bold Eagle, tired of playing games,
rode off through the green hills to survey the buffalo. The
country was black with them. Deer, antelope, and other animals were also in abundance. Overhead flew flocks of geese
and ducks while pheasants darted out in every direction from
under their horses.

"It is a rich land, full of game," Cougar Woman said.

"No wonder the People of the Pheasants live in such lux-
ury! They have permanent lodges and game at their doors."

Looking down on the winding river, they could see another village of earth lodges nestled among huge cornfields.
Most of the people were in the water—some swimming, others paddling around in tublike boats.

"Do you think that is another village of the People of the
Pheasants?" Cougar Woman asked.

"Perhaps they are our cousins the Earth Lodges. We have
come a long way."

"You are probably right. Let's return and tell Tall Bull
what we have seen."

"Look—those women in the water swim like fish." Bold Eagle enjoyed the picture of frivolity.

"These people on the river seem to like swimming as much as we like riding horses. The water is warmer than ours—almost too warm."

"And not as clear."

They turned their horses and went back the way they had come, taking several pheasants with their bows. Raven or Sweet Grass would roast them on a spit over the fire until they were done.

When they arrived at the village, something was different. On the far side of the village, across from the Absaroke tepees, there was much activity. Strange rectangular dwellings were everywhere. White men in blue uniforms patrolled the hills. Two big black guns were aimed down at the Indian camps.

Bold Eagle and Cougar Woman found Tall Bull standing in front of his lodge watching. "The white soldiers do not trust us," he said. "They know we have come in peace but it makes no difference. They think we do not keep our word as they do not keep theirs. They have put weapons above us so they can fire down on our people."

Tall Bull was angry, his face drawn in a scowl. "Perhaps we can do something to their guns," he suggested. "We cannot risk letting them kill our people by mistake."

Cougar Woman stood beside him looking at the big black guns.

"The white men would not shoot us without reason," Bold Eagle said.

Tall Bull remained unconvinced. "I cannot take a chance on the white man's intentions—tonight we will spike their big guns. I will do it myself, with help."

Then Tall Bull turned and went inside to smoke and think. They were to meet with the commissioners that afternoon. He would say something about their lack of faith.

Later in the afternoon, Tall Bull and Weasel Bear were taken to the tent camp along with their advisors. Cougar Woman and Bold Eagle followed Tall Bull. Behind Weasel Bear were Two Suns and two other warriors. Six white men sat around a table and looked up as the two chiefs with their advisors were brought in. It was hot in the white men's tent even though the sides were rolled up. The white men's interpreter stood up and addressed the assembled Indians. Some of the tribesmen sat outside listening to what was going on. White soldiers posted on the hills as well as soldiers guarding the tent of the commissioners all marched back and forth.

"We have come from Congress, the seat of the government of the new United States, to meet you, the head men of the Crows, to give you peace and to offer you the opportunity to receive the favor and protection of the United States that you, your people, your wives and children may be happy and free and know the blessings of the new changes coming over this land that you inhabit.

"We sincerely wish you to live as happily as we do ourselves, and to promote that happiness as far as is in our power, regardless of any distinction of color, or any difference in our customs, our manners, or particular situations.

"Congress, which is the sovereign of the United States, wants your friendship. We want none of your lands, or anything else that belongs to you, and as an earnest of our regard for you, we propose to enter into articles of a treaty perfectly fair in every way. We expect you will speak your minds freely and look upon us as representatives of your father and friend, the Congress, who will see justice done on your behalf. You may now retire and reflect on what we have told you, and let us hear from you tomorrow before the sun is high."

The interpreter sat down and the white commissioners began to talk among themselves, ignoring the Absaroke delegation, which rose as one and filed out.

Weasel Bear and Tall Bull went to Weasel Bear's tepee to sit outside and smoke in the fading sunlight. Each was deep in thought. Tall Bull watched the activities of the white soldiers as they patrolled the hillsides near the big guns. So they wanted peace with his people whom they called "Crows." He was in favor of peace, but what would the Absaroke have to give the white man and what would they get in return? He would not regard a strange body of white men as his "father," no matter what power they exerted or what favors they granted. Theirs was the power of numbers and superior weapons, not of greater intelligence. That was given by The One Above who put his red children on the earth to care for it. The trappers in Absaroke country were examples of how the white man acted. They were not satisfied with taking only what they needed; they had to have everything in sight. Tall Bull relit his pipe and spoke to Weasel Bear.

"Are you unhappy with the white man's big guns?"

"That is the way of the white man. He deals in such a manner with what he does not know."

"Perhaps. But if he is frightened, he could kill our people."

"True. But I think the white man means well. It would be good for our people to sign a treaty with him. Then we will be protected and our lands will remain our own." The old chief had a faraway look in his eyes. He did not like fighting. He was tired and wanted to trust the white man to live up to his word.

Tall Bull was worried. The white men had no reason to train guns on them. No, he would not sign a treaty of friendship with a rattlesnake; he would sign nothing under the threat of guns. He stood up and walked to his tepee where he would talk with Cougar Woman and Bold Eagle. Then he would spike the guns so they would be useless against his people.

Cougar Woman was silent as Bold Eagle made his thoughts known to Tall Bull. "I think we should see what the white man has to offer us. If it is in our favor, I think we should accept. We have little to fear from the trappers or the few whites in our country. If too many come, we will chase them out or kill them as the Pecunies do."

"Do you think the white man's word is good?" Tall Bull questioned.

"I do not know."

"If you do not know, how can you sign a treaty? It will be nothing but a worthless piece of paper."

"If the treaty is good, we will lose by *not* signing it. The paper can prevent what you fear will happen. Papers, like guns, are the way of the white man."

"We could ambush thousands of their soldiers without losing a warrior if they tried to take our mountain valley."

Cougar Woman had enough of Bold Eagle's passive attitude. "No white man can fight as well as one of ours," she interjected. "Even though they outnumber us, we can win if we use their weapons."

Tall Bull's mind was made up. "First, I shall take some warriors and go up to the big guns. Then I will listen to what he has to say once more. If it is to our advantage, I will agree to it. But I will honor nothing if one white man breaks its terms."

Cougar Woman and Bold Eagle were silent. There was no more to be said. They would follow him to disable the guns. Tall Bull would do what was best.

In the middle of the night, Tall Bull led Cougar Woman, Bold Eagle, and eight other warriors up the hill toward the cannons. They spread out in the darkness and worked their way further up behind the guards. Tall Bull ordered that no one be killed—only temporarily silenced until the guns were spiked with thick stakes he had made to plug them up.

The warriors reached the top of the hill and crept up to the mounted guns. Tall Bull began to look one over, carefully figuring out where to plug it so it wouldn't fire.

Suddenly, a bugle sounded. They were surrounded and a voice blared out: "Do not move or cause your warriors to shoot. Go back to your tepees. Meanwhile we will hold your chief in his lodge until our next meeting."

Tall Bull knew he was in trouble. His people below were unprotected. He did not want to risk having them slaughtered. Surrendering himself, he watched his warriors, under escort, go back to their tepees. Then he went to his lodge, where two soldiers stood until dawn when they were relieved by two more.

The commission met as it did the previous day. Tall Bull and Weasel Bear sat in front of the six white men, who appeared grim. The soldiers lined up outside the tent and were more in evidence than before.

Tall Bull spoke. "We do not want to talk peace under the sights of your guns. Indeed, is it not strange to talk peace when we have not yet been at war? My warriors have not killed white men as our neighbors the Pecunies have. We do not bother them, except to take a horse here and there as payment for the thousands of beaver they take from our streams. But pointing your big black guns on our village is not a way of talking peace."

Tall Bull stood straight as a lance, looking into the eyes of the whiskered white men who shifted restlessly in their camp seats. His voice reverberated throughout the tent. As the interpreter spoke, he wondered if the man repeated his words correctly.

When the interpreter finished, Tall Bull continued. "We will listen to the message you bring us from your Congress, but our hearts are not open to those who would threaten us for no reason."

Weasel Bear stood. His voice sounded like crackling leaves. "My brother is hard in his judgment. We will listen and see what the white people want from those who have never been at war with them."

Tall Bull sat down with an impassive face. He was smoldering inside from being caught at spiking the guns. He
wondered how the soldiers had learned of it.

The white interpreter was spelling out terms of the
treaty. "The Congress wants our friends and brothers, the
Crows, to swear fealty to the United States, the new nation
on this continent. We know our brothers are in the habit of
trading with our white neighbors to the north. This is con-
trary to the interests of the United States, and we ask that
the Crows cease all trade of this sort. In its place, to assure
our brothers of money and goods, the United States will
regulate through its own offices all trade with the Crow
Nation.

"We are aware, and Congress knows, that bad white
men cause trouble among our brothers. We ask further that
the Crows do not avenge any of these wrongs but instead
refer them to the proper authorities of the United States
government—in this case, the Army of the United States.

"In return for these acts of fealty to the new and powerful United States, the Congress will give certain acts of
kindness to its brothers, the Crows. Goods will be sent at
specified times to ease the burden of survival in a harsh
environment. The new United States pledges its friendship
and help to its brothers forever."

The interpreter sat down. The white commissioners cir-
culated the document, each one signing it. Then the soldiers
brought in loads of goods to be distributed to the people as
indications of friendship.

Weasel Bear stood up and the excited hum that covered
the room hushed. "I accept your terms of friendship with
the United States and our father and friend, its Congress.
The Absaroke people have long been friends with the white
man and are happy to have this opportunity to prove it."
He walked to the pile of goods and looked through the
blankets for one with bright colors.

Tall Bull was silent. He saw no advantage to be gained in dealing with the United States under these terms. For years, the French had been coming to their lands. This would mean they could no longer trade with them or with the English. It took justice out of their hands. No, he would not appeal to the white man every time a wrong should be set right. That would solve nothing.

He stood up facing the commissioners. His voice was grave. "I do not sign treaties that benefit only one party. I do not wish to sign until the white man proves his good intentions. The white man is good at talking. We are an independent nation and it is our right to trade with whomever we please. We will not give up our old friends for untried new ones."

With that, he turned and walked out of the tent. Everyone was silent as the Absaroke mountain band rose and followed him. They would pack up and leave.

When Tall Bull arrived at his tepee, a strange horse was outside. Inside, Raven was feeding an ancient chief—his cousin Black Moccasin, chief of the Earth Lodges, the People of the Willows. Tall Bull embraced the old man.

"Welcome to my tepee. You have come at a poor time. We are leaving to return to our home. The white man's treaty is no good for us."

Black Moccasin signaled for Tall Bull to sit beside him. He offered him his pipe. "It has been many moons since I have seen you, my son. You are a wise chief. I am glad the snows of age are on my head and I will soon go to the Beyond Country where things will be like they once were here. The white man brings many changes that are not good for our people."

The old man's white hair fell below his shoulders where it was wrapped in otter skins. His face looked like weathered parchment, but his light-colored eyes were sharp and penetrating. "You almost succeeded in dealing with the white man's guns last night, but you were betrayed."

Tall Bull moved closer to the old man. "You know?"

"I know most things. These neighbors of ours, the People of the Pheasants, have spies. You will find that their chief White Wolf Cub, who tries to please the white man and use him to his own profit, told them of your plan."

Tall Bull felt his anger rise like a grass fire fanned by the wind. He could not kill White Wolf Cub, but he would take revenge on the People of the Pheasants.

"I will call for rain," he said angrily, "and drown their crops. They will learn that betraying people of their own skin has more serious consequences than befriending the white man."

Tall Bull took his medicine bag and opened it on the ground in front of him. Black Moccasin took his own bag from his belt. Raven gave Tall Bull a small drum, which he started to beat in a slow, throbbing rhythm. In high, wavering voices the two chiefs sang to the spirits:

Bring rain to earth, oh Father,
Bring rain to us now.

The drum echoed through the small camp. Cougar Woman, who was outside packing their belongings for the return trip, wondered what her father was doing. She also wondered who owned the fine horse tethered beside Tall Bull's. Whoever it was, was inside, too.

Bold Eagle rode up and hailed her. "Look at the black clouds gathering. We are going to get rain. It might be better to wait until the storm is over before leaving. This country sometimes has floods."

"Tall Bull is not ready," she replied. "He has a visitor."

The clouds rolled over like great white stallions and charged across the sky. Thunder rumbled across the plains and the sky grew darker. Then large drops of rain spattered in the dry grass of the village. Soon the rain was pelting down and streams were rushing through the gullies. Cougar Woman and Bold Eagle ducked inside the tepee and sat back away from Tall Bull and his guest, Black Moccasin.

Tall Bull put away his drum and gave Raven the sign to pack up. "We move as soon as the rain stops," he said. Then he turned to his young warriors. "Come forward and meet your relative, Black Moccasin, chief of the People of the Willows."

"We rode to where we could see his village surrounded by cornfields," said Cougar Woman. "We are glad to meet the great chief."

Black Moccasin smiled and rose. He stood with his hands on Tall Bull's shoulders and looked into Tall Bull's face. "It will not be long, my son, before you will join me in that other world we speak about so often. Until then, lead your people as you have been doing. The white man means you no good. I know you must lead your band home, my son, so I shall take your greetings to my people."

He walked to his waiting horse, mounted with difficulty, and turning it toward the south, he rode off into the slackening rain. Floods swirled the gullies and the corn crop near the stockade stood battered, deep in water, ruined.

Tall Bull's band packed up and before long was on its way home. Tall Bull, Cougar Woman, and Bold Eagle rode in front with the Wolves out ahead. Weasel Bear's people were distributing the gifts of the white man. They would stay several more days while Weasel Bear basked in his new importance as treaty signer. The white men had given him a silver medal to wear around his neck.

Tall Bull was grave as he led his people back to their mountain stronghold. Perhaps the white man would win, but why hasten the day? It was more important that his people get ready for winter. The time for the hunt was near.

With affection, he looked over at Cougar Woman and Bold Eagle. They were strong warriors who could lead, but how they would cope with the whites when he was gone, he did not know. He knew only that his time was close. His medicine told him so.

9

Journey to the South

THE SCAFFOLD HOLDING TALL BULL'S BODY STOOD ALONE AGAINST the vastness of the grassy plains. Below it the body of his best war horse lay where Cougar Woman had sent an arrow through its heart so that Tall Bull would have his beloved beast in the Beyond Country. Raven and Cougar Woman had put out his best weapons and food to help him on his journey. Then they had cut off their hair and rent their faces until the blood streamed down their chests. Sweet Grass and Bold Eagle had joined in the grief, cutting their hair and wailing. The whole village vocally mourned the loss of its chief.

Now, a few days later, Cougar Woman sat on her pony beside the scaffold looking at the horse carcass already torn by wolves and buzzards. She felt deep pain and loss. Her father had gone and she was alone. She felt her throat constrict with grief and she fought to keep back tears. She was done with grieving outwardly, although she would always remember them bringing the battered body into the tepee after the fatal hunting accident. She had not seen it happen but heard from Bold Eagle that Tall Bull's horse had snapped a leg in a prairie dog hole and thrown him in front of the stampeding herd. He did not suffer long. His old bones were crushed like brittle wood.

She reflected that the night before he had foreseen his death. He had talked to her with a grave expression on his face, telling her of his long life and of the many places he had visited and the coups he had counted. He learned through all of them, he told her. Finally he said, "Look at me and see my face. All men have flesh. All men have hearts. All men know what death is. I shall soon know what I have been seeking." When he saw her expression change to concern, he added, "Stand firm. Remember your heart and all I have taught you."

Then he stopped talking. He was leaving early to go after buffalo. She was patrolling the hunt as a Fox and would not be riding beside him as she had in the past. She wished he would not go, but he meant to do it one last time. Who was she to stand in his way?

She turned her gaze from the carcass to the line of travois and horses as the people moved away from this camp of sadness. They were loaded with buffalo meat and hides to make their long winter easier. The travois of the village moved out of her vision over a hill. She could see the dust and hear the dim noises drifting on a stiff breeze. It felt cool on her neck with her hair cut short.

She took one last look at the scaffold. Next spring she would return and gather his bones. Then pointing her horse toward the disappearing Absaroke, she galloped off to take her place among the honored men at the head of the line.

Several weeks later, when the band had settled into its winter camp, Cougar Woman sent Sweet Grass for Bold Eagle. When he came, she met him in her tepee and they sat in front of the fire that Raven was feeding. She passed him her pipe and watched as he smoked. Raven and Sweet Grass brought food and put it in front of him. Then they went to a corner of the lodge to play a game of dice.

"Before Tall Bull went to the Beyond Country he told me of many places he had been in his life," Cougar Woman said, watching Bold Eagle for any reactions. He was smoking and looking into the fire. "He told me of his trip to the south where strange plants with spines grow and where people are small and live in white clay houses with many families."

"I have heard of such a place."

"He told me of a great trade fair at a place called 'Taos,' where red men from the south bring slaves to sell and where beautiful horses are traded."

"Is this place still there?"

"I do not know, but I would like to see some of the things my father spoke about. He also talked of places where snows do not come but the sun shines all winter and the land is hot and dry."

"What would you do?" Bold Eagle was curious. He had not heard Tall Bull tell of these wonders, but he wanted to see them. He waited for her answer. She was puffing on her pipe, her mind far away.

"I would go and see these things."

"Would you go alone?" Bold Eagle was hoping she would invite him along. He wanted to see houses of clay and snow-less winters.

"No, I would like company. Then we can take some of those fine horses Tall Bull mentioned, and scalps and captives if it pleases us."

"I shall go with you and we will send word to Crooked Nose, who is a good boy and would like to go also. Perhaps their women are beautiful."

They started their journey in the early morning of a brisk fall day when the golden leaves of the aspens covered the trail under their horses' hooves. They took several good horses with them—to trade, to carry goods, and to use as spare mounts. Crooked Nose and Bold Eagle rode behind Cougar Woman as they left the winter camp. Already the peaks were covered with snow. They rode for hours till the sun was high. Then they came to the Stinking Water and followed its banks, traveling south until they met the great north road that their ancestors' ancestors had followed at the beginning of time when they first came into this land.

Cougar Woman was deep in thought. Her dream the night before had shown her a white village crowded with colorful people. In the background, a high snow-covered peak watched over it and a stream ran from its cloud-shrouded heights through the village, dividing it in two. In her dream she had taken two women from a bowlegged man who was trying to sell them. He was dirty with unmanageable short hair that flew over his head. He wore a knife and knee-high boots of animal skin and a breechclout. He followed her, saying things in a strange tongue.

She looked around at Bold Eagle and Crooked Nose. She thought one of them should begin scouting ahead so they would not run into unexpected trouble. She reined in her mare and signaled to Crooked Nose. "Be our Wolf and see what lies ahead," she said. "Do not be rash. We have a long way to go to the land of the trade fair people."

He smiled with delight at being given this privilege, and galloped out.

Bold Eagle rode next to Cougar Woman. He was dressed in his capote and wore two feathers in his shortened hair. He had a white man's gun on his saddle as well as his bow and shield. She had left her own stolen rifle with Raven and Sweet Grass. Both of them could use it, although chances of their having to were slight. Winter was not far off and few enemies would venture deep into the mountains. By the time spring came, she hoped to be back.

Cougar Woman and Bold Eagle rode together in silence thinking about what lay ahead. When they made camp that night, they still did not converse. There was not much to say. Both felt the loss of Tall Bull and knew his spirit was riding beside them. What they would find, they did not know— some answers to their problems perhaps, enjoyment, new horses. Their medicine was good and would guide them.

For days they traveled near the great jagged peaks west of the Stinking River, avoiding the Grass Lodges. Eventually they came to the land of the Black Lodges, who lived in mountains somewhat like their own. Game was abundant, and water plentiful, unlike conditions in some of the arid country they had come through. Relieved to be in the mountains again, Cougar Woman killed an elk and they ate the roasted meat.

In the cool of the late fall night, Cougar Woman was awakened by the sound of a snorting horse. She took her knife and, with Bold Eagle, crept toward their horses. Crooked Nose, on guard, was leaning against a boulder sound asleep. The horses were restless and the nickering grew more pronounced. Cougar Woman saw a figure leading her horse away. She ran silently until she could throw her knife, which went deep into the man's back. He fell forward without a sound. She waited, watching the shadows. Beside her, Bold Eagle strained his eyes to pick up any movements. There were none. Satisfied, they moved to the fallen man. He was a Black Lodge warrior. She retrieved her knife and horse. Then, not bothering to scalp him, they covered his body with brush to conceal it. They did not want the Black Lodges after them.

Returning to camp, Bold Eagle kicked Crooked Nose awake. He opened his eyes in bewilderment.

"While you slept we almost lost all the horses. Foolish boy!" Bold Eagle snorted in disgust.

They wanted no trouble and lost no time getting out of the area. The mountains here were snowcapped, and one morning they woke to snow flurries and a light dusting all around them. Wearing winter clothes, they continued south and were soon rewarded with sunshine as they came out on a broad plain split by a deep canyon that followed the bed of the river that made it. Despite the snowcapped peaks, the ground was clear and the sun very warm. A well-used trail led to the foot of the peaks, where they saw people of all kinds going about their business.

"We must be near the trade fair," Cougar Woman said after seeing some Cheyenne warriors drive a herd of small but very fine-looking horses by them. There were fields of crops, too, near the main trail. White men with heavy oxen pulling large squeaky-wheeled carts passed them; black-haired, agate-eyed children were riding in the carts and pointing at the strange sights. The whole place buzzed with activity. Small mud huts dotted the area. Ahead they could see a church spire with the black robes' medicine on top. Several miles to the south, another of the white men's churches stood with twin towers. As they rode closer, the activity seemed to increase. Then they saw the white communal dwellings of the local Indians.

"Look," Cougar Woman said, "there are the many-family houses Tall Bull spoke of, stacked one upon the other."

Bold Eagle was intrigued. "No wonder the people are small. To live in one of those and climb up and down ladders they would have to be." He took off his heavy capote and shrugged his huge shoulders. Bold Eagle was a big man, well over six feet tall. Crooked Nose, next to him, was over six feet tall also, and was dressed in decorated buckskin. Along with Cougar Woman, who was close to six feet herself, they made a fine looking trio. Their hair was just long enough to braid. Both Bold Eagle and Cougar Woman wore their hair that way, with eagle feathers hanging from the braids. Cougar Woman had added otter skin strips to hers.

As they rode toward the entrance to the pueblo, people stopped to stare at them. The scalp decorations fringing Cougar Woman's and Bold Eagle's shirtsleeves added to the awe they inspired. These two at least were great warriors and everyone wondered what they wanted to trade. Because of a law enforced by the Mexican government that no fighting would take place in the area surrounding the Pueblo de Taos, things were generally quiet. Inside the pueblo walls the Taos people enforced their own strict laws governing all who came to trade.

Numerous Indian groups pitched camp around the pueblo. The Comanches had come from the south with many horses and captives to sell. They were eager to complete their trading, as winter was coming and they wanted to move to their big camp near the Arkansas. Their village here extended over a large area, and they raced their horses and gambled right under the eyes of the Mexicans, who were afraid to do anything about these wild wolves of the southern plains.

Cougar Woman and Bold Eagle camped in a cool grove of trees outside the walls of the pueblo. They instructed Crooked Nose to watch their horses and goods without falling asleep. Then the two of them inspected their trade goods. There were two fine buffalo robes and a shirt tanned to pure white and decorated with red quills. Sweet Grass spent hours working on it and Cougar Woman had promised to trade it for something from the southern tribes. They looked over their horses and decided that if they saw any they liked better, they would trade for them.

Once inside the pueblo, they found stalls with hagglers waiting to sell things like finely woven cloth in bright colors and baskets interlaced with the tightest weave they had ever seen—so strong and taut they would hold water. Behind one stall piled with sheepskins, Cougar Woman saw a huge, brightly colored bird. Its reds, greens, and yellows fascinated her. It sat on a stand and watched the people, occasionally scratching its head with a leg or preening its feathers with a large, yellow hawklike beak. It made croaking noises. She pointed the bird out to Bold Eagle.

"He looks like he's from the Beyond Country," she said. "Listen to him chatter. It sounds like a tongue from another world."

"He is beautiful with his long tail feathers. They would make fine decorations. Do you think he is good to eat?"

She shrugged. "I do not think he is used for eating."

They walked farther into the busy fair and came to an Indian from the south with a beautiful horse. It was standing beside him quietly. The horse's tail was almost white and fell to the ground in silky waves. Its mane was the same color, but the body was darker and sleek as a spring deer's coat. They looked at the horse in admiration. Bold Eagle felt the animal's flesh and inspected its hooves. The horse was young and in fine shape. Bold Eagle pointed to the horse and, in sign language, asked the Indian how much.

The small bandy-legged man shook his head no and turned away to stare at a group of Comanches with horses. Cougar Woman surmised the horses were not broken though they were sturdy stock, wiry, and looked as though they would take a lot of abuse.

Bold Eagle was still admiring the small man's beautiful horse. "I would like that one," he said to Cougar Woman. "Do you suppose he would sell it to me?"

"He didn't seem interested," she replied, watching the Comanches herd their fractious animals into the small corral.

"Perhaps he will change his mind. I will ask again." Bold Eagle went up to the small dark man and pointed to the horse and at himself. "I want that one. What will you take for him?"

The man listened politely as Bold Eagle offered him a buffalo robe for it, then a buffalo horse. The man made signs saying he had few buffalo in his country and his people sometimes ate horses, so what did he want with a buffalo horse? One horse tasted like another.

Bold Eagle was appalled. He couldn't imagine eating horses; they were his friends. The thought of eating a horse, even an old one, made him want to purify himself. He stared in surprise at this strange red man from the south. Then he asked him where he was from.

The man smiled agreeably and launched into elaborate signs of plants that grew as high as hills and had knives all over them. He picked up a handful of dust and blew it toward the south. "I live many days to the south near a great river," he explained. "My people roam through land as dry as dust and inhabited by rattlesnakes. We eat roots and wild game, which is abundant, even though water is not. Some of our mountains have thick forests on their sides, but in the valleys no trees grow. Frequently we go even farther south to lands where green birds live. There we get captives to use as slaves."

Bold Eagle was fascinated. He answered the man with a description of his own habitat. "I live in high mountains to the north of here where snow already lies on the green grass of the valleys. We hunt buffalo—that is why I want your horse. It looks like it would be a fine one to train."

Cougar Woman noticed the little man glancing at some Comanche captives. Two of them were women—small like the man himself and wearing clothes made of skins.

"I got this horse from a Mexican soldier and brought it to trade for my woman, who is being sold by the dogs that stole her from me four days ago. Already they have passed her around among themselves—now they want to sell her. I want her back. She is a good woman. We have been together many years. If she is sold, I will never see her again. If no one buys her, they will kill her because they cannot be burdened with a captive."

The man looked unhappy.

"Do you really want that horse?" Cougar Woman asked Bold Eagle.

"Yes, I will buy the woman back for him. Then he will trade with me." Turning to the man, he asked, "What is your name?"

The man pointed to his chest. "I am called Nachise. I am Apache." Then he turned his attention back to the women to be sold by the Comanches.

Cougar Woman and Bold Eagle walked toward the Comanches and their captives, one of whom was much younger than the other. "The young one would make a good woman for my lodge," said Cougar Woman. "It might be easier to buy them both."

"Look at the children," Bold Eagle exclaimed, pointing to a group of dirty, raggle-taggle youngsters being herded by their Comanche captors. "Who will buy them?"

"I don't know. They are too small for work. Some look white."

Bold Eagle nodded. Great yelling and shouting attracted their attention to an open area. The Comanches were leading the children to it, and people were gathering around. "Perhaps the big trade begins," said Bold Eagle, heading toward the circle.

The Comanche guards put the children in the center of the ring. Then a dark-faced Indian stood up and started talking, pointing at the children. No one in the audience responded, so he pulled a young girl to him and ripped off her rags. Then he spun her around in front of the jeering crowd. He ran his grimy hands over her body, making obscene motions. The girl struggled to keep from crying out. She tried to hide her face. When no one would buy the scrawny child, the dark-faced Comanche shoved her back to the center of the ring and grabbed a boy of about the same age. He stripped the boy and paraded his scarecrow body up and down the circle, again making obscene gestures to get his point across.

Bold Eagle and Cougar Woman watched, fascinated. They did not understand the language, but the gestures were unmistakable. Suddenly a fat white man in a black, decorated suit raised his hand and yelled something at the Comanche. The Indian shoved the naked boy at him and caught a small bag of gold the white man threw. The man led the quivering boy away. The Comanche repeated his words and actions with the other children. When there were only a few left, the crowd began to disperse. The Indian slaver was furious about not selling all of his children. Several other Comanches came up suddenly and surrounded the remaining youngsters. Then two men pulled knives and swiftly cut the children's throats, walking away as the bodies fell to the ground.

Cougar Woman said, "The Apache was right. They do not keep captives they cannot sell. We should get the women quickly if you wish to have that horse." Cougar Woman started off after the Comanche warriors. Bold Eagle followed her, wondering what he would have to trade to get them.

They hailed the Comanches. The warriors turned and looked at the tall northerners approaching them and smiled in greeting. The Absaroke, they knew, were brave warriors and fine stealers of horseflesh. Many years before, they had sneaked into the heart of their huge Comanche-Arapaho camp and stolen prize horses out of the stockade—an admirable feat.

"Greetings. We have been admiring your captives," said Bold Eagle, pointing to the two cowering Apache women. "They come from the far south, do they not?"

The Comanche leader walked up to Bold Eagle, who towered over him. "They are from the land of the spiny plants that grow without water. Do they appeal to you?"

"Yes. My sister and I wish to take them back home with us. They would please our people."

"They will not cost much. We do not want them. We have had our pleasure, and now they are nothing but mouths to feed."

"I can give you a good spotted horse for them. We brought one from the far northwest, where they raise the best horses of all."

"So?" The Comanche looked interested. "Where is this horse? I would like to see him."

"I will bring him to you here when the sun is high. Then, if you like him, he will be yours and the two women mine."

"It is done." The Comanches laughed at their good bargain—a fine horse for the two flea-bitten women who were not even good where women should be.

Later that day, Bold Eagle and Cougar Woman led their good Nez Percé horse to the trading area. The Comanches were waiting with the two unhappy women. Their misery stemmed in part from thoughts of being slaves to these tall mountain people in cold lands where the wind froze the breath as it came out of you.

Bold Eagle led the horse around in a circle. It was a fine animal with spotted hindquarters and a long mane and tail. The Comanches liked it immediately.

"It is a good beast," said the Comanche leader. "Such an animal is rare among our people. I shall have it and you may have the women." He pushed the captives at Bold Eagle. "You are getting the worst of this trade. They are no good."

"The horse is yours," said Bold Eagle, handing its rope to the Comanche. The man sprang on its back and thundered away.

Signaling the captives to follow him, Bold Eagle walked to the spot where he had last seen Nachise. The little man was sitting by his horse beside the clear stream that flowed through the pueblo. He jumped to his feet when he saw who Bold Eagle brought with him.

"Nachise, I will trade this woman for your horse."

Nachise's eyes brightened. Then he asked suspiciously, "But what of the other woman? She is of my wife's blood."

"She belongs to the one I travel with who needs a woman in her lodge to work, make clothes, and do other things women do."

The Apache's black eyes lit up again. That was not a bad fate for his wife's relative. These mountain people looked wealthy. "I will give you my horse for the woman, although she is not worth it. It is a high price to pay." He wanted to bargain a bit longer, but he was glad to get his woman back.

Bold Eagle was delighted with his horse. In no time at all he was riding it at full gallop across the open fields around the outskirts of the pueblo. Cougar Woman ran her Pecunie mare beside him.

"It is a fine animal, Bold Eagle, but it will need training before you can use it to hunt buffalo," she told him.

"I will teach it quickly." He urged the horse to top speed and turned it this way and that, testing its ability. He was pleased. A Nez Percé horse was not unique among his people, but this beauty with its curved neck, great spirit, and odd coloring was a treasure—a breed set aside for chiefs of the Beyond Country.

"Tall Bull would have liked this horse," he said to Cougar Woman as they returned to their camp. "It is worthy of the best warriors only. Where do you think the Apache got it from?"

"He said he stole it from the Mejicanos." She imitated the Spanish pronunciation of the word. "We'd better not show it around too much."

"You are right. I am ready to return to our mountains anyway. I have had enough of trading."

"First I must get something for Sweet Grass. Do you think he would like a green bird?"

"Yes, but I do not think the bird could survive in our climate. It is from warmer lands."

"Then I shall take him some of those woven baskets that hold water. Surely he has seen nothing like them. The pots with designs are also nice and would be a help. A woven cloth might even appeal to him. The colors are bright."

"Sweet Grass is your problem, not mine. I shall take Swift Water Woman a basket." He got off the horse and motioned to Crooked Nose, who was being good about obeying his elders.

"Watch this animal with your life," he told his brother. "It is special." Then he began to pack their camp goods while Cougar Woman made a last trip to the pueblo. She took the white shirt and a robe in case she found something she liked.

Getting the baskets and pottery was easy. A Pueblo artisan was delighted with the finely beaded buckskin shirt and piled her up with baskets and pots that nested into one another. The Apache woman, who had followed her, agreed to carry the trade goods. Cougar Woman was pleased with her helper.

As they headed back to camp, Nachise appeared out of nowhere, grabbing Cougar Woman by the arm and pointing excitedly to a group of uniformed white men. He motioned her to take him to the horse he had traded to Bold Eagle, so together they ran back to the camp where he and Crooked Nose had just finished packing up their goods.

Nachise ran up to the horse and pointed toward the pueblo, then made the motion of slitting his throat. Bold Eagle understood. He leaped on the horse's back and, with Crooked Nose, moved quickly toward the north, taking several other horses with them.

Cougar Woman collected her things. Then leading a horse with the Apache woman riding in the rear, she followed him. Nachise had made it clear that the white men were looking for the thief who stole a ranchero's prize horse.

Cougar Woman glanced toward the pueblo with its snow-capped peaks looming overhead. There was no sign of pursuers. She urged her horse to a gallop, eager to get back to her people. She would catch up with Bold Eagle tomorrow.

The next morning, Cougar Woman woke to several feet of snow covering the thick fir trees surrounding their camp. She moved out of the brush shelter the Apache woman had made, and while the woman cooked some deer meat, she gathered the horses and brought them to camp. The snow had stopped and the world around them sparkled. She wondered how Bold Eagle was making out and how far ahead he was.

Looking up in a tree, she saw a tribe of the chickadee people. "Do you know how far ahead Bold Eagle is?" she asked one as it chattered and flitted in the snow-covered pine. It came close and looked at her. Then, one by one the entire tribe of little birds moved north to another grove of trees.

"Even I know he is to the north," she said as she walked back in the shelter. The air was cold and crisp and the breeze crackled through the brittle branches. The Apache woman gave her some meat, which she took hungrily. They would not eat again that day.

Later they packed the remaining deer meat, which was already frozen. Then Cougar Woman, wrapping her buffalo robe about her, got on her horse and began the long journey home. The Apache woman, enveloped in blankets, led the packhorse and rode behind Cougar Woman. Running away, she knew, was futile, and besides she was not averse to serving this one who had saved her from sure death. She could still feel the bruises she suffered at the hands of the Comanche men.

They rode all day through the snow. Ice balls collected on the horses' hooves. In late afternoon they came to a broad valley where the snow was light enough for the grass to show through. Herds of elk, deer, and buffalo had congregated here and were foraging for what feed they could find. Cougar Woman hauled her horse to a stop and pointed to the herds.

"Do you have animals like this in your lands?" she asked the Apache woman.

The woman shook her head no as she stared in awe at the vast numbers of beasts.

Cougar Woman smelled the air. There was smoke in it. Accustomed to the cold, pure air of the high country, her nostrils twitched. It might be Bold Eagle and Crooked Nose waiting for them. Cautiously, she moved down into the herds, her big horse shouldering some of the animals aside as it pushed along. Getting closer to the source of the smoke,

Cougar Woman stopped, put her hands to her mouth, and yelped like a coyote. Then she waited, listening. All she could hear were the munching sounds of the animals about her. A few minutes later she let out several quick yelps. This time answering howls came back. She put her weapons away and moved ahead. She knew it was Bold Eagle waiting for her.

Wanting neither trouble with the whites nor to lose his fine new horse, he and Crooked Nose had reached this valley quickly. They had made camp in a cave that protected them from the cold winds and snow. Early that day they had shot a fat buffalo cow so they would not starve before arriving home. Following the valleys north would take at least several weeks—many more if they ran into bad storms.

Crouching behind a boulder, Bold Eagle watched to be sure Cougar Woman was the one who answered his call. There was always a chance it was an enemy, or a real coyote. There were numerous wolves and coyotes about, preying on the weak and diseased animals of the herds. He had seen cougar signs, too. He caught sight of Cougar Woman riding ahead of the Apache. It was good she had a young, vigorous helper for her lodge. Bold Eagle stood and waved. Cougar Woman galloped over.

"It is good you are here," she said. "I wondered how you got so far ahead."

"It is safe here."

They walked into the cave, and the Apache built a fire pit while fanning the old fire to keep them warm.

That night Cougar Woman dreamed she was riding alone in a vast desert. There were mountains in the distance that turned purple and kept moving farther from her. She rode until she was thirsty. Then she saw a lake, fresh and sparkling, but as she tried to ride there, it, too, kept moving out of reach until she was exhausted. At last the spined plants around her turned into huge trees and she was back home in her beloved mountains. Tall Bull waited for her. He sat beside her in front of a great blue tepee and they smoked together.

"Beware," he told her. "The one to look out for now is a red man of another tribe."

Then Cougar Woman awoke. The smell of Tall Bull's pipe was in her nose. She sat upright. What did he mean? She went to Bold Eagle, who lay by Crooked Nose at the entrance of the cave. Kneeling beside him, she whispered, "Bold Eagle, my brother, wake up and listen to my dream. I do not understand it."

His eyes opened, and with wonder in them he reached for her and pulled her to him. "Is this what you want, like all women?" he asked as he engulfed her in his bearlike embrace.

She struggled mightily. "No. I no longer want a man that way. My medicine forbids it now, and it does not appeal to my nature. If you want a woman, take the Apache, but do it gently or you will feel my wrath. Let me up."

He released her and quickly recovered from the realization that he wanted her. "I am sorry," he said. "I was half asleep, dreaming of women. My medicine forbids me to touch you." He paused to collect himself further. "I do not want your woman. She does not attract me."

He listened to Cougar Woman recount her dream, then sat and scratched his head. "I, also, do not know what it means. We face death always from our enemies."

"Tall Bull warned me. I hope I will know what he means." She went back to her corner and lay awake thinking.

The next morning they packed up and began the long trip home.

10

The Last Arrow

Cougar Woman sat on a hillside overlooking the busy Absaroke village. It was a place favored by Tall Bull, who used to sit and think in this spot before going to meet with the honored men. So, too, was she contemplating things to be decided.

The noises from the village reached her on a breeze that left a cold touch on her cheek. She looked lovingly on this scene; it had changed little since her girlhood. Life had been good to her here. The Absaroke people had been kind—more than kind—and so she must weigh carefully the decisions she would make that could affect their lives and their futures.

Last week she had gone to the Mountain of the Cougars to seek medicine for guidance. But instead she found a dead cougar lying on the trail, a white man's bullet through its head. She had not seen the white man. If she had, she would have killed him and placed his scalp with the cougar, or maybe even his heart, as an offering to the fine beast who died for no reason.

She had gone on up the mountain to the spot she had used many years before when she'd had her first contact with the cougar. She fasted for three days, hoping her medicine helper would come. Finally, on the third day, as she lay dozing in the warmth of the late afternoon sun, she heard a call. Cougar Woman sat up. At the edge of the rock stood a cougar, its golden eyes looking upon her sadly. Then in a deep voice it spoke to her.

You have seen what the white man heaps upon our Mother Earth. It is just beginning. He destroys more and more of her bounty.

"I have seen some and heard more of the wastefulness of the whites," Cougar Woman said.

Yes, and their greed will also affect your people as it has done already in the lands to the east. This will be the beginning of something evil that will affect all life on earth.

"What can be done?"

Nothing—at least not in your lifetime or in many lifetimes to come. There is little you can do to alter the course of the whites. Some of your people will survive and be better off than others because they did not fight the white man. There is little to choose between. Those who would live proudly can but die proudly when life is attractive no more.

The cougar stared at her as if it would spring away at any moment.

Your time is near, it said. *Do what you can for your people. At least you will not live to see the sadness inflicted upon them through the hatred and duplicity of the whites.* With that, it bounded into the rocks and disappeared.

Cougar Woman sat quietly on the mountain for a long time. Regardless of what was done, her people could not win. Was it not better to fight and die as a proud warrior than to be driven into corrals by the whites?

The Absaroke were a small tribe. Alone they could do nothing. Only with allies could the red man hope to be strong enough to protect what was given by The One Above. But the

Absaroke had few allies. She would therefore go to their enemies, her blood people, on a peace mission. Certainly the Pecunie chiefs would see the wisdom of joining together in a union of tribes against an enemy of everything they held dear. Surely they would put aside their conflicts and petty quarrels until they were safe again. With this thought, she left the Mountain of the Cougars and returned to the village, planning to meet with some of the honored ones to discuss the future.

That night the council met in her tepee. Four honored men were there, including Bold Eagle. After they had assembled, and Sweet Grass, Raven, and the Apache woman had moved to a corner of the lodge, Cougar Woman lit the ceremonial pipe. Puffing on it a few minutes and blowing smoke toward Father Sky and Mother Earth, she passed it to Bold Eagle on her right. "The time has come for us to decide," she said. "Will we seek allies among our enemies—the Pecunies, the Dakotah, and other tribes who face the same foe? Or will we become allies with the whites and, in attempting to save some of this land that is so dear to us, suffer what they choose to give us?"

The pipe was passed around and the warriors sat gravely considering the choice they must make.

Bold Eagle spoke first. "I think the way of peace lies open to us. If we befriend the white man, surely he will treat us with honor." He was not really sure in his heart, but he felt his people had no chance if they fought against overwhelming odds and firepower.

Swift Bear, the oldest warrior present, drew himself up with effort as he pronounced his opinion. "I do not think we can trust the white man. I cast my vote for war." He did not see how the white man could win against all the tribes fighting together, although he did not see how he could trust his lifelong enemies either. Only dead Pecunies and dead whites could be trusted.

Cougar Woman spoke again. "If no one here objects, a delegation will go to the land of the Pecunies to see if they will fight beside us. For years they have seen that we do not kill white men in our country as they do. They may not trust us. But I shall go myself. I would like to see the people from whom I came and the land that was once my own. I will send a messenger to their chief tomorrow and arrange a meeting for the next moon."

Crooked Nose was chosen as messenger and he went with a message of goodwill. The Pecunie chief, White Otter, was interested and opened the way for the peace mission to come to his village near the Medicine River. Preparations would be made to receive the Absaroke people and a great feast prepared.

Early in the summer Cougar Woman and a delegation of ten went north to the Pecunie village. She and Bold Eagle rode together at the head of the group. "We will see how it is to be in the land of my birth," she said. "I have often wondered."

"Yes," replied Bold Eagle. "However, you are welcomed not as a lost Pecunie but as an enemy coming in peace to talk about war." He was not sure this was the right thing to do. The Pecunies had been their enemies too long. "The wolf cannot change its shape," he added. "I hope this is not true of the Pecunies."

"We will see."

They rode for days, wondering at the lack of Pecunie warriors once they moved into their enemies' territory. They followed the Medicine River to a large valley. There Cougar Woman rode out on an overhang beside the rocky trail. Below her she could see hundreds of Pecunie tepees. The village was arranged in three circles alongside the river.

"If we were coming to steal horses, we'd get many good ones," Bold Eagle said, pointing to the large herd grazing in a meadow by the river.

Cougar Woman laughed. "I have never been here before. Have you?"

"No, I did not know about it. They are well hidden." He turned his horse back to the trail and she followed, looking at the toothlike granite peaks that seemed to surround the valley.

"In country like this, we could hold the whites back for years."

Bold Eagle nodded in agreement. Then they continued down the mountains to the Pecunie village.

At the foot of the trail they were met by a party of honored men from the Pecunie Nation. The principal chiefs rode four abreast, their lances and shields in hand and their feathered warbonnets trailing almost to the ground. They rode to about five yards from the Absaroke delegation and came to a stop. Behind them, feathered Pecunie warriors, many of whom had tangled with these Absaroke leaders over the years, wheeled and raced their horses, showing off their strength and prowess.

The head chief, White Otter, raised his arm and the action came to a dusty halt. Then he addressed the delegation. "Welcome to our village. You have come in peace and we greet you in peace. As our guests you are welcome in our lodges. We ask you to pitch your tepees here beside the river. Our people are preparing a feast of roasted elk for you."

Cougar Woman, flanked by Bold Eagle and Swift Bear, addressed the Pecunies. "We are pleased to be welcomed to your beautiful valley. Like our own mountain valley, it is full of game and beauty, precious to both our hearts. It is because of this that we have put away our age-old enmity toward you: We feel that only together can we hope to defeat the white man, who threatens us all and would take what we love most. Many times in the past I, as well as my warrior brothers, have met the brave Pecunies on the warpath. We have stolen horses from them as we have from our other neighbors, and they have from us. It is our way. But even this shall change if we are to protect our way of life. We come in peace."

The Pecunie head chief listened well to the Absaroke woman he had heard so much about, and he nodded in agreement as he listened. "You are welcome," he said. Then, raising his arm again, he wheeled his feathered war horse and galloped back to the village with his party at his heels.

The Absaroke visitors set up a small camp—ten lodges quickly erected by the women. Then they waited to be called for council. Cougar Woman lay on her buffalo robe in the lodge while Sweet Grass, permanently crippled from his beating, made their camp comfortable. He had a sense of dread about this meeting, although he could not pinpoint why. "I do not like being here in the nest of our enemies. There is something dark and mysterious about it." His voice was tense.

Cougar Woman had grown used to his frequent pronouncements. "Everything will be all right," she said. "This meeting is as much for them as for us." She had not told him about the cougar, for fear of upsetting him.

"It would have been better if you had not allowed Running Fox to come along. I feel he will do us no good."

"He has earned a place, even though he purchased his medicine." She disliked Running Fox, too, but what could he do to her now? She could handle him. If the cougar was right, her time was close at hand, and nothing could alter the way of The One Above. Anyway, she would not live to see the sufferings of her people. The cougar had said so and she was glad.

Deep in thought, she smoked, shutting out the village sounds as well as Sweet Grass's grunting as he settled in. She didn't trust the Pecunies. However, they must see what would come.

The next day White Otter, followed by several lesser Pecunie chiefs and war leaders, came to the Absaroke lodges to lead the visitors to council. He was dressed in his finest shirt, fringed with ermine tails and decorated with scalps and porcupine quills. His warbonnet, filled with eagle feathers for each coup he had made in his long career, reached to his heels. He carried a carved pipe with turkey and eagle feathers fluttering from its long stem.

The Absaroke were not to be outdone. They had dressed in their finest outfits. The white deerskin shirts and leggings—the pride of the skilled Absaroke women—were magnificent; they were decorated with porcupine quills and scalp and animal fur fringes. They, too, wore eagle-feathered warbonnets and underneath, their long black hair was sleek and silky.

The council between the two enemy peoples took place in a grove of cottonwood trees by a clear cold stream that flowed into the Pecunie camp. A semicircle of Pecunies sat facing a semicircle of Absaroke chiefs.

The Pecunie chief White Otter spoke first. "Since the beginning, when our people came down from the north, we have had one enemy. My father, his father, and many before him have brought back Absaroke scalps so our women could dance around them and vent their feelings for those of our blood who were killed by Absaroke warriors. Today, this is forgotten and we greet the Absaroke delegation in peace. What we will do another time cannot be considered. We are all children of The One Above. Even our enemy, the white man, is a child of The One Above, although sometimes we have children we would rather be without. I believe this is how The One Above feels when he looks upon his white child. Let us hear from the Absaroke chiefs and we will listen to what they have to say."

White Otter sat down and commenced to smoke his pipe, which was passed around. Cougar Woman, as the leading chief in the peace delegation, stood up. The only noise was the gurgling of the swiftly moving stream. In a steady voice she said: "The great chief White Otter has spoken well. I shall not repeat how for many years the Absaroke and the Pecunies have fought each other—stolen each other's horses, taken each other's scalps. It is a dream of every Absaroke warrior, just as it is of every Pecunie warrior.

"Now into this world has come a foreign element. It is a destructive force much greater than any one of us alone. It threatens not only our way of life but also the survival of our Mother Earth. For years, since the first white man came to our country, the Absaroke people have refused to kill him. We have been peaceful. He has set up trading posts and sent hunters and trappers into our country. His men have killed our elk, deer, and buffalo, and have trapped the beaver out of our streams. Our enemies, the Pecunies, have killed white men who come into their country and try to trap their beaver. The white man knows this but still he comes. Who is to say the policy of killing is working better than ours? I do not know.

"A new white post has just been built where the Elk River meets the Big. It is a large fort in a rich buffalo range and will provide a way for the white man to push further into our lands. The trader there will dispense whiskey to our people if we allow it. This in itself may prove worse than bullets.

"The white men will bring strange diseases which, like the illnesses in the east, will wipe out our people by the thousands. Only we can stop them, but we cannot do it alone. The white men are like hailstones in a mountain storm. Because of their number, we may never defeat them, but I think we can keep them out of our country. We can defend the land given to us by The One Who Knows Everything—if we do it together. That is why we have come to talk to you, the Pecunies. Your land adjoins ours and you control the passes across the mountains to the far sea that the white man seeks."

Cougar Woman sat down. The pipe was passed and she smoked in silence, reflecting upon what she had said. Bold Eagle looked at her in admiration. An aura of strength seemed to come from her body. The Pecunies had been listening spellbound to this well-known woman chief whom many of them hated and feared. Her scalp would be a fine prize for any warrior.

White Otter rose. "We will consider what you have to say and meet here tomorrow at this time." He turned and walked toward his tepee. His chiefs followed him.

Cougar Woman looked at Bold Eagle. "What do you think they will do?"

"I don't know, but remember, we are only one Absaroke band. We must try to convince Weasel Bear to join the Pecunies if they agree to an alliance."

"That can be done. His people favor keeping things as they were, even though he does not." She was sure of that. Tall Bull, after their meeting in the land of the People of the Pheasants, had suggested this was so.

"If we cannot agree with our enemies, we will have to trust the whites. After all, the Pecunies have been our foes since before anyone can remember. The whites have not and they may need friends who know the ways of the tribes who fight them." Bold Eagle, although content to go along with her, still felt that an alliance with the whites would be preferable to one with their lifelong enemies.

That evening, the Pecunies opened up the roasting pits and hauled out the meat. The Absaroke joined in the feast and there was much visiting back and forth between the tribes. Everyone was in good spirits.

Running Fox, feeling especially good, sat next to one of the Pecunie chiefs. The Pecunie spoke of the council.

"Your chief talked of things that are close to the hearts of us all. She may be right—the only way to defeat the white man is to put away our grievances and join together."

"My chief?" Running Fox gave a derisive laugh. "I hate her. How can you listen to one who rides a Pecunie racehorse stolen from a chief, and who years ago killed three of your finest warriors in a fight over that same horse near the trading post on the Bighorn River?"

The Pecunie started in surprise. His eyes darkened and a scowl came to his face. "She is the one who stole the black mare? Then she killed my brother who tried to get it back."

Running Fox laughed. "She has killed so many Pecunies I cannot count them. Perhaps your brother's scalp dangles from her shirt." He was enjoying this. The more trouble he could make for her, the better.

The Pecunie got up and left Running Fox. He could feel the rage boiling within him. His brother, a chief, son of White Otter, was killed by this Absaroke woman. He knew White Otter would allow no breaking of their word. The Absaroke were to be welcomed in peace and they would go in peace. He would kill her, but not in the village, where his father would know of it.

The next day, the council met again in the prearranged spot. Each of the lesser chiefs spoke of how he felt, and after many hours the council disbanded to meet again the following day.

That evening Bold Eagle and Cougar Woman sat in her tepee. Sweet Grass served them some food and listened to their conversation. He felt very gloomy. Something bad was brewing but he did not know where. His powers since his beating by the Dakotah were not as strong as before. Now he wished he had them. He feared something would happen. He prayed silently and made an offering by throwing some meat into the fire, but he had the horrible feeling nothing could help. He moved up beside Cougar Woman. When she looked over at him, he spoke.

"You must leave. Do not stay for the meeting tomorrow. Go tonight so no one knows you are gone. I feel something terrible will happen."

"I cannot run in the middle of the night. Besides, they will not dare kill me when we are welcomed in peace. No man with honor would do that, and White Otter is an honorable chief, even if he is a Pecunie."

"Please go!" He turned to Bold Eagle, "Make her go. She is in danger here."

Bold Eagle said nothing. He could not force her to go if she refused.

"I will leave after tomorrow's council. I cannot go before."

Sweet Grass did not know what else to do. If it was the will of The One Above, so be it. He left the tepee and wandered about in the dark.

White Otter spoke at the next day's council. "We have considered the words of your chief and all of you, and we feel it is right. We will put away our war clubs and greet the Absaroke as brothers in our common fight against the white man."

Cougar Woman was pleased. "We will send leaders from our two bands to meet with you, White Otter, and your chiefs when the geese fly south. Then we will plan what we shall do to defeat the white man. There are others we should also talk to who might join us in our fight." She sat down.

Immediately, she heard a commotion behind her, then a cry. Turning, she saw Sweet Grass fall, a knife stuck in his back. She rushed over and knelt beside him. His eyes were open and he struggled to speak. "Running Fox betrayed you," he said, and then he slumped in her arms, dead.

Cougar Woman looked around and could see no sign of Running Fox. The chiefs were all standing and watching.

White Otter was very upset. This was a bad omen. He looked at his second son who was standing nearby with a strange expression on his face. His son had come to him last night and told him of his conversation with Running Fox. White Otter had instructed him to put it out of his mind and heart. That day was past. White Otter wondered about his son and if he had put it out of his heart. His son could not have done this. He had been sitting beside him in the council.

Cougar Woman and the rest of the Absaroke packed their things and mounted their horses. She was taking Sweet

Grass's body home and she was going to kill Running Fox. Cougar Woman felt waves of sadness roll over her for her friend of many years who she believed had died saving her life. She remembered him as Dreaming Boy who had befriended Captured One Who Rides Like the Wind.

The Absaroke rode back up the rocky trail out of the Pecunie valley, with Cougar Woman in the lead. Bold Eagle rode beside her, disturbed and confused. The rest of the delegation, except for the missing Running Fox, brought up the rear.

After a short while Cougar Woman stopped the line and, leading the horse bearing Sweet Grass's body, rode back to Swift Bear. "I am going after Running Fox. Bold Eagle will come with me. Please lead the people back to our village and give Sweet Grass's body to Raven. I will be there as soon as I can."

"Be very careful. Running Fox knows you will come." Swift Bear's lined face was grave.

Nodding, she turned her horse and galloped back to Bold Eagle. "Will you ride after Running Fox with me? I shall take his scalp to put beside Sweet Grass's body."

Bold Eagle said nothing. He knew how furious she was but decided that before she put aside her reason, he must tell her what Sweet Grass had said to him.

"Sweet Grass died because he overheard Running Fox plotting with one of the Pecunies last night to kill you. Do you remember our trip to the trader for my capote years ago? You killed White Otter's first son there, and his brother wants to avenge his death."

She listened, realizing that Sweet Grass had tried to warn her. Running Fox had fled and prepared a trap. But she must kill him—only then could she look upon Sweet Grass's scaffold in peace. "I will kill Running Fox," she said, riding off at a fast pace with Bold Eagle in pursuit.

They followed Running Fox's trail for two days. It went

through the mountains and came out in country strewn with huge boulders. They had seen no sign but the hoof marks of Running Fox's horse, and those were not easy to follow over the rocky terrain. Suddenly Bold Eagle waved to her, pointing. In front of them down in a depression, they could see two horsemen—one was Running Fox. Cougar Woman got off her horse. She reached for her medicine bag and opened it. Taking some cougar heart powder, she smeared her forehead with it. Then she scattered some to the wind.

Looking at Bold Eagle, who was putting his eagle feathers on and drawing red stripes across his face, she said, "I must tell you, beloved brother, that I found a dead cougar on my last visit to the mountain. It may have been a sign that the power of my medicine is gone. We shall soon see."

Before he could answer or try to stop her, she leaped on her horse and started down the rocky trail, intent only on killing the man she had hated for so long. In her hand she held her weapons ready to use when she got within range.

Behind her, Bold Eagle rode, grim and fearful for his life-long friend.

When they got to the open area where they had caught sight of Running Fox, they found the tracks of another horseman joining him. The two rode back into the country of giant rocks. Cougar Woman paused to look around, then walked her horse, carefully looking for signs of her quarry.

They followed Running Fox's trail as it wandered through the rocks. Suddenly it seemed to vanish.

She stopped, listening for the sounds of hoofbeats on rock, but heard nothing. Then there was a swish, a breeze by her ear—an arrow narrowly missed her neck. She threw herself off her horse and rolled behind a rock. Bold Eagle was beside her. She pointed to a large red boulder shaped like a tree trunk, and ran toward it. Bold Eagle went the other way, both of them circling until they could close in on Running Fox. Cautiously, she peered around the rock in time to see

Running Fox stand up and aim his bow at Bold Eagle. She
shot him in the heart. His hand released the arrow marked for
Bold Eagle and the bow clattered on the rocks before his body
collapsed in death.

Cougar Woman looked for Bold Eagle. Not finding him,
she hastened toward Running Fox, eager to take his scalp,
when Bold Eagle shouted to her.

Cougar Woman pitched forward as an arrow struck her in
the back, then she dropped facedown in the red dust. She knew
nothing except the cold creeping into her limbs. Somewhere in
her fading memory, she could see the golden eyes of the cougar
and hear its voice telling her that she would not live to see the
misery of her people. Far away, she heard Bold Eagle's voice
crying to her in great sorrow. It was fading, fading until all that
was left was the fiery light in the cougar's eyes.

Horrified, Bold Eagle had seen Cougar Woman, in her
frenzy, forget the second rider and rush toward Running Fox.
He had seen the Pecunie rise from behind a rock and shoot
the arrow that killed her. He knew it was too late to save her.
Bold Eagle then killed the Pecunie, whom he recognized as
the son of White Otter.

Even if Tall Bull had been there with his strong medicine,
he could not have pulled her back. Bold Eagle cradled her
head in his lap and sobbed aloud in grief, tears dropping on
her dead face as he called her name to the peaks. After a long
while, he picked her up and walked to his horse.

He held her body in his arms as he rode back into the
mountains looking for a place where the eagles nested. Hours
later, he came to a high peak with an eagle flying overhead.
He got off his horse and walked, still holding her in his arms,
the two horses following him. His eyes, misty from the tears
that flowed, searched for a deep fissure in the rocks. At last he
found what he wanted. He wrapped her body in a buffalo
robe and set her gently in the crevasse. Then he climbed farther toward the eagles. Taking his bow, he shot a golden eagle

as it flew nearby, and he set the dead bird beside her. Then he carefully walled up the opening with rocks.

Bold Eagle got on his horse. He took her horse, suspecting that to kill it would only lead people to her grave. He would return now to the place of her death and scalp the Pecunie dog as well as Running Fox. Then he would leave their bodies to the wolves and the birds of death.

As his horse slowly picked its way down the rocky trail, Bold Eagle's body shuddered with grief. She was gone and with her all hopes of the Absaroke ever joining the Pecunies. They could not be friendly with a tribe that had deliberately killed one of their leaders when peace was being considered. He would see to that while he lived. Alliance with the whites would be the path their people had to follow now. Nevertheless, he would not be there to see it. He would rather ride alongside her forever in the Beyond Country than live without her.

He looked at the blue sky. The eagles had gone and he knew it would not be long before he would be with her again. His medicine eagle was already dead beside her. He had killed it to keep her company until he could join her in the land where the buffalo would never disappear.

About the Author

Jane E. Hartman, ND, PhD, DIHom, DHM, a former college professor, is a workshop leader, ordained minister, and award-winning author of books for young people and adults. Four of her children's titles on animal behavior and the environment have won recognition as Outstanding Science Books for Children by the National Science Teachers Association and the Children's Book Council. Among her twelve fiction and nonfiction books are two novels about Native American women—*Cougar Woman* and *Hoku and the Sacred Stones*—several Native American texts including *The Original Americans,* as well as a guide to energy techniques entitled *Shamanism for the New Age.* Dr. Hartman has spent more than a decade living and writing in the Southwest.

About the Cover Artist

Dee Lambert, a native of New Mexico, is a fine artist specializing in watercolor-transparent, watercolor-opaque, egg tempera, casein, pen and ink, and pencil techniques. Her work focuses on the indigenous people of the Southwest and is displayed in solo shows, group exhibitions, galleries, and private collections. She is a recipient of the Western Writers of America Golden Spur Award, Futures for Children Premier Collection Award, and several prizes at the Bicentennial Show in Pueblo, Colorado.

ORDER FORM
Books by Jane E. Hartman

Quantity	Title	Amount
_____	*Cougar Woman* (Unabridged Edition) $16.00 each	_____
_____	*Hoku and the Sacred Stones* $4.95 each	_____
_____	*Shamanism for the New Age: A Guide to Radionics & Radiesthesia* $15.95 each	_____
	First-class shipping and handling ($3.25 per book)	_____
	TOTAL AMOUNT ENCLOSED	_____

Quantity discounts available.

Please contact your local bookstore or mail your order, together with your name, address, and check or money order, to:

AQUARIAN SYSTEMS INCORPORATED, PUBLISHERS
PO Box 575
Placitas, NM 87043